Aubrey is a lot of things—clumsy, an enforcer for his coven, a babysitter when needed. He's also stubborn, which is a good thing when it comes to Oren, the guy he has his eyes on.

Oren isn't blind. He can see how gorgeous Aubrey is, and more importantly, that he's a man Oren could easily fall for. He can't afford it, though. He's a conclave enforcer, and he's in charge of finding the dhampirs who are killing the vampires in town one by one. He doesn't have time to waste, even if it's with Aubrey.

Aubrey knows all of that, but he doesn't care. Oren won't catch the bad guys by working twenty-four seven. He and Oren have different opinions, and they clash together only for Oren to push Aubrey away again.

The dhampirs are still on a killing spree, though, and Oren is terrified something will happen to Aubrey. He's already lost one person to the dhampirs.

He won't lose a second one.

Stubborn Fangs
Copyright © 2020 Catherine Lievens
ISBN: 978-1-4874-2992-8
Cover art by Angela Waters

Published by eXtasy Books Inc or
Devine Destinies, an imprint of eXtasy Books Inc

Look for us online at:
www.eXtasybooks.com or www.devinedestinies.com

Stubborn Fangs
Life with Fangs Book 5

By

Catherine Lievens

Chapter One

After spending most of the day guarding the coven, Aubrey had barely sat down on the couch when Andrew found him. He groaned when he saw Andrew's face. He could tell from his friend's expression he wouldn't like whatever Andrew was about to ask.

He closed his eyes and tried to ignore Andrew, but Andrew stood there until Aubrey looked at him again. "What do you want?" Aubrey asked.

"Falkner wants to visit Darren."

Aubrey groaned again. "Why? The man was planning on killing him. Why would he want to see him or be his friend?"

Andrew shrugged. "I have no idea, but I won't try to change him. He's a good man."

"If you ask *me*, he should be less of a good man and think of his safety more."

"You know he won't do that. Anyway, he needs someone to go with him."

Aubrey was right—he didn't like what he was hearing. "Why don't *you* go with him?"

"I have something to do. I would if I could, but I can't."

"What about Richie?" Those three were together. Surely Richie could go with one of the men he loved.

Andrew shook his head. "He's working with James. He tried to get out of it, but you know he doesn't like it."

Because James needed to be able to control his shift and his werewolf. An out-of-control werewolf was never a pleasant thing to have on your hands, but especially so in a vampire coven.

Aubrey sighed. "Can he go later once one of you is back? I just sat down."

Andrew's expression was apologetic. "I know. I would ask

someone else, but I trust you with his safety."

Aubrey knew Andrew wasn't doing it on purpose, but he was saying the exact things that would get Aubrey to get his ass off the couch and go with Falkner. He liked that Andrew trusted him with one of the men he loved. Most of the coven trusted him, but Andrew and Falkner had been Aubrey's friends since they'd arrived. He wasn't their best friend — they'd been each other's best friend for so long that he wasn't sure anyone could change that, or at least, he hadn't been sure until Richie had arrived — but he was close to them, and he wanted them to be safe and happy.

He dropped the back of his head against the couch and closed his eyes again. "Fine. I'll go with him. I still think he's nuts, though."

"You and me both, though I understand why he's doing this. He feels close to Darren because they're both dhampirs. I still don't like it, though."

That still stunned Aubrey. He wouldn't have known, since when he'd met Falkner, Falkner had already been a vampire. It changed nothing for him, but he knew a few coven members had grumbled about Fyfe allowing Falkner to stay with them. Personally, he didn't care. He wouldn't have cared even if Falkner was a purple cow shifter. Falkner was Falkner, and Aubrey loved him for who he was, not what he was. Besides, they already had two werewolves living with them. What did it change if a dhampir lived there, too? And there was Adrian. Aubrey loved him, even though he had no idea what to do with him most of the time, and even though Adrian was a vampire-werewolf hybrid. For whatever reason, Ignatius and Oscar had decided Aubrey was the perfect babysitter for their adopted son, and he couldn't get out of it, no matter how much he wanted to.

Maybe that was because he didn't *actually* want to. He might not know what to do with the baby, but he loved that kid.

He rose from the couch and stretched. "Where is he?"

Andrew looked relieved. "Still upstairs. I'll tell him you're waiting for him. I'll also tell him not to spend too much time there. I know you need some rest, and I'm really sorry I'm asking you to do this."

"But if you weren't asking me, he would go alone, and we both know that's a bad idea." Bad was an understatement.

Andrew looked away, clearly embarrassed. "I know I shouldn't be doing this. He's an adult, and he can protect himself."

"But he's just been attacked by a bunch of dhampirs, and you can't shake that fear. I get it. You don't have to explain, and I'm more than happy to go." Aubrey paused. "Well, I would have been more than happy if I hadn't just spent an entire day guarding the coven, but I'll survive." Besides, maybe Aubrey would be lucky enough to see Oren.

Ignatius worked for the conclave, and Oren was his team leader. That man was so hot that Aubrey hadn't been able to stop thinking about him, and he would always be grateful to James for being accused of murder and having Oren and his team come after him.

He doubted James felt the same way, though.

He suspected Oren didn't like him, but that didn't matter, at least not much. It wasn't like they were getting married or anything. Aubrey just liked having some eye candy to look at while Falkner was busy with his murderous friend, and Oren was more like eye caviar or champagne, as far as he was concerned. He was delicious to look at, and Aubrey couldn't look without wanting to lick him from head to toe.

He should probably stop thinking about that kind of stuff when he was with Oren, though. He was pretty sure every single thought showed in his expression, which would explain why Oren always looked like he'd rather be eating nails than spend any length of time with him.

Andrew patted Aubrey's shoulder. "Thanks. I'll tell him to come downstairs."

"And I'll be waiting." Unfortunately.

Since he had a little time, Aubrey headed to the downstairs bathroom. He washed his face and made sure his hair looked okay. He didn't know if Oren would be there, but since Ignatius was in the house and not out on a mission, there was a good chance he would be. Oren wouldn't be happy to see Aubrey—he never was—but Aubrey was convinced there was more to the distaste Oren seemed to have for him.

He didn't mind that Oren wasn't crazy about him. He might want to have sex with Oren, but he could take no for an answer, and he could limit himself to watching the guy. It was a pity, but Oren wasn't the first guy who didn't want Aubrey that way, and Aubrey could deal with it. He'd done so plenty of times.

When Aubrey walked into the entrance, Falkner was bouncing on the balls of his feet. "Thanks for doing this.".

Aubrey rolled his eyes. "You know Andrew asked me?"

"I do. I told him I could go alone, but he won't let me out of his sight if I'm on my own. I think it's ridiculous, but if it makes him feel better, who am I to argue?"

That was the kind of relationship Aubrey wanted. Falkner was fine on his own, but he understood that Andrew was worried, and he didn't mind doing this for him. It was a minor thing, a small gesture that showed how much Falkner cared for Andrew. Aubrey wanted the same, whether it was with Oren or someone else. He honestly didn't care. He wasn't in love with anyone at this point, although he couldn't deny he had a crush on Oren. But he knew nothing would come out of it, and that was fine. But as it was, he'd been single for a while, and he felt like he would never get laid again.

He huffed and turned his attention back to Falkner. "Let's go," he said.

Aubrey almost turned the car around only five minutes away from the house because Falkner opened his mouth and asked, "Are you hoping to see Oren?"

Aubrey had done his best to hide his crush. He didn't want Oren to be embarrassed, and he didn't want people to tease him. "I'm sorry?" he asked, keeping his focus on the road.

"You don't have to hide it, not from me. I won't make fun of you. There's nothing to make fun of. I was just trying to make conversation and to check in on my friend."

Aubrey sighed. "Fine. I might have a little crush on him. It doesn't mean anything, though."

Falkner was smiling widely when Aubrey glanced at him. "It might not mean anything, but maybe it could."

"No. He's made it clear that he's irritated by me, and that he doesn't want to sleep with me."

"Did you ask him?"

"No." Aubrey could too easily imagine how that conversation would go. Oren would probably die of laughter or something.

"You can't know for sure, then. Why don't you give him a chance?"

"Because I'm pretty sure he would have made his move if he wanted anything more with me."

"Again, you can't know that. How could you? How many times have you spoken to him?"

"Not many," Aubrey had to admit. "Not because I didn't want to. I've asked him out a few times, but he always says no." And then Aubrey had stopped. He could see when he wasn't wanted.

"Maybe it wasn't that he didn't want to, but rather, that he was busy, or that he thinks he needs to focus on the job. A lot has been happening around town recently, and Oren's team is right in the middle of it. Why don't you try talking to him again? It might not lead to anything, but if it does, you'll be happy."

Aubrey wasn't looking forward to being rejected once again, but maybe Falkner wasn't wrong. Maybe he needed to talk to Oren when things were a bit calmer—when he could have a nice conversation with him instead of a quick chat in a hallway.

Aubrey wasn't sure, but knowing he had an option made him look toward this visit with a smile. He still didn't understand why Falkner wanted to talk to Darren, but that didn't matter, because Aubrey was going to talk to Oren.

"The rise in vampire deaths in the city is worrying," Milford said.

Oren wanted to answer *no shit*, but he knew better. Milford took himself seriously, and this was a serious matter, so instead of being snarky, he nodded. "It is. There's been a sharp rise in the number of deaths, and I don't like it."

"I doubt anyone likes it. Do you have any idea what's going on?"

"I don't have any proof, but I suspect dhampirs."

Milford's eyes widened. It made Oren wonder if the man ever read the files and reports Oren and the other team members wrote. Probably not. "Dhampirs? Are you sure?"

"Pretty much, since we broke up a group of them recently."

"Right. The people in our cells. Why haven't they all been executed?"

"I'm not the right person to ask that," Oren said even though he'd a hand in it. He still wasn't sure it was the right idea, but having at least one dhampir in their jail might help them. Darren wasn't friendly, but he could give Oren insight into dhampirs, and that was what they needed right now.

If Oren had a choice, he would use someone else, someone who was a vampire now instead of a human. He would use someone who knew what being a vampire meant, but he couldn't afford to do that. Smart dhampirs were in hiding, especially if they were vampires now, and he wasn't about to reveal their names to anyone, least of all Milford. Who knew what the man would do with that knowledge? Probably try to get them imprisoned for one reason or another, and it wouldn't end well.

"I see. So you're sure we need them here?"

"Well, they were part of a dhampir group. They might know about other dhampirs, other groups of them. So yes. I'd say the few we still have are useful."

"Good. I want you to keep me up to date on this."

"I will." Oren kept the entire conclave up to date. Milford wasn't his favorite person to deal with, though. He wasn't the smartest, and Oren suspected he didn't care about the conclave or the vampires the conclave was supposed to protect. He'd become part of the conclave because his father had been before him, but he wasn't good at it. There wasn't much Oren could do, though. If Milford wanted to talk to him, then he would. He was part of the conclave, whatever Oren thought about that, which meant he was Oren's boss.

Oren was grateful when the meeting was over. He let Milford leave, knowing he probably had lunch planned or something like that. He didn't care. As long as it distracted the man, he wasn't creating trouble for Oren and the other conclave teams. The last thing they needed was to be distracted when they were dealing with groups of dhampirs trying to take over the city and kill as many vampires as possible.

He sighed and closed his eyes, rubbing the bridge of his nose. He was tired, and his day had only begun.

He needed to do something. His team had taken out a

dhampir group, but there were more out there. He was sure of that, but he had no idea where to start looking for them. With one of their groups gone, they knew the conclave was after them, and they'd gone into hiding. They still came out every so often to kill vampires, but they were even more careful, and so far, no one had been able to find them.

Oren rose from his chair and headed out. He wanted to talk to Darren, who was their best bet to find out what was happening. The human was still snarky and didn't like to talk to anyone, least of all Oren, but he'd become more compliant. Oren suspected it had a lot to do with Falkner's visits, and while he didn't understand them, he wasn't about to protest, not when they gave him exactly what he needed.

He wasn't surprised to see Darren looked angry when he was guided into the interrogation room where Oren was waiting for him.

"I was watching TV," Darren whined. "I'm going to miss the big reveal."

"Do I look like I care?" Oren asked.

"Why *would* you care? But I want to know who's the father of Lucy's baby. I won't understand anything that happens next if I don't find out."

Oren ignored the whining. "I have a few questions for you."

"You always have questions for me." Darren sat on the chair in front of Oren on the other side of the table and crossed his arms over his chest. "I don't like you. I don't like your questions. I don't want to be here."

He sounded like a child, and in a way, he was. He might be a dhampir, but it wasn't because of anything he'd done. He'd been born this way. He was young, so very young next to Oren, and nothing would ever change that. He was also still human, which was probably one of the reasons he was behaving this way.

Oren felt pity for him, and he also felt sorry. He couldn't show any of that, though, so he kept his expression neutral. "I have some questions about dhampirs."

Darren rolled his eyes. "You always have questions about dhampirs. Let me repeat what I already told you. I don't know who the other group leaders are. I wasn't even a leader, not really."

"But you were in charge of your group."

"Kinda? I mean, not really. I was the one who got the orders from the guy in charge of our group, but it's not like I could force anyone to follow them. I was just the guy who got the orders, told the others about it, and went along with them. I'm no one's boss."

Oren knew he was telling the truth. The group of dhampirs he and his team had arrested had been disorganized and young. It took a lot of discipline to do what the dhampirs were doing. Oren doubted the groups killing the vampires were all as young as Darren's had been. They wouldn't have so many victims.

"Tell me more about the person who gave you your orders," Oren said.

Darren sighed, sounding put out, but he answered. "There's nothing much I can tell you. All the dhampir groups are isolated. That way, if one of them is taken down by you guys, we won't be able to tell you where to find the others."

Oren had suspected that much. It made sense. Oren couldn't deny they were smart, no matter how much he disliked them and what they were doing. "The person who gave you orders?"

"Again, nothing much to say. I never met the guy. He always called, and I answered. I'm pretty sure other groups answer to him, but I can't tell you that for sure. I do think the dhampirs are organized, though. It was kind of obvious in the way they recruited us and tried to train us."

That was new, and Oren leaned closer. "What do you mean *organized*?"

Darren shrugged. "A bit like you guys. I never met another dhampir group, but I know some work together at times. But there's someone up there who was controlling all of us. It makes sense. I don't know who makes the decisions, though, but everything points to them being organized. We obey orders, but there's only one person who has the entire picture."

That worried Oren. He'd suspected as much, but he'd hoped he was wrong. It was better to deal with small, disorganized groups of dhampirs who didn't know what they were doing then to deal with someone who had a lot of manpower and who wasn't afraid to use them—and to sacrifice them.

He couldn't get anything more out of Darren, and he wasn't surprised. He'd already gotten more than he'd expected, so he left Darren in the interrogation room, knowing he'd probably go back to his cell and his TV. That was okay. He'd been helpful, and he would be helpful again.

Oren left the hallway where the interrogation rooms were and stepped into the wide entrance, groaning as soon as his gaze stopped on Aubrey. He was there with Falkner, no doubt to see Darren. Oren knew what would happen now. Falkner would go to the interrogation room to have a chat with his dhampir friend while Aubrey would hang around in the entrance. That was a problem, because Aubrey wasn't discrete, and he wasn't a quiet guy. The last time he'd been there, he'd thrown a sword that hung on the wall to the floor, and the noise had made everyone turn around. He'd blushed, then waved and grinned at Oren.

Oren didn't like attracting attention, and that was what would happen with Aubrey around.

Aubrey had noticed Oren coming from the area where the prisoners were interrogated, and he grinned at him. He saw Oren roll his eyes, but he didn't care. He knew he was annoying at best, infuriating at worst, but so far, Oren hadn't told him to fuck off, and he hoped that wouldn't change.

Oren strode toward Aubrey and Falkner, and Aubrey couldn't help but let his gaze run over him. *Damn.* He was a fine piece of human being, or rather, of vampire. Oren was tall, and his shoulders were wide enough that Aubrey could hold on to them without a problem.

Aubrey wasn't ashamed of his own body, and he kept it well trained because he was one of the coven's enforcers — the head, in fact — but he couldn't deny Oren was very much different. He was even taller than Aubrey, who was six feet. Oren had to be at least six foot three, maybe six foot four. Aubrey couldn't tell, but he kind of wanted to drag Oren closer and measure him — with his tongue.

Oren was also blond. Aubrey had always had something for blonds, and Oren wasn't any different. He was everything Aubrey liked, packaged into a body that was to die for, and Aubrey licked his lips once Oren was standing in front of him and Falkner.

Oren noticed, and he rolled his eyes again, something he seemed to do fairly often when he was around Aubrey. "Falkner," Oren said.

Falkner smiled at him. "Hi. I'm here to see Darren."

"I suspected. He's still in one of the interrogation rooms. I just talked to him."

Falkner frowned. "Is everything okay?"

Oren looked around. He looked like he wasn't sure how to answer that, and Aubrey waited, wondering if he would say anything. Aubrey and Falkner didn't have a right to the information, and Oren probably *shouldn't* talk to them, but they'd been there when the dhampirs had been arrested, or rather, Falkner had been. He'd been friends with Darren. He'd wanted to be close to him and the other dhampirs because he knew where they were coming from. He'd been like them once.

Instead, they'd tried killing him. Aubrey still didn't understand why Falkner was so bent on becoming Darren's best friend, so he'd stopped trying. Still, Falkner was a vampire now, and he could probably help Oren. His involvement wouldn't do any damage. Darren already knew him. He wasn't even trying to kill Falkner anymore, which was a definite improvement.

Oren rubbed his face. He looked tired, and Aubrey wondered how much he would glare at him if he suggested he go to bed—possibly with him. "There's been another murder," Oren said.

Falkner frowned. "The dhampirs?"

"I don't know, not for sure. Probably, though."

"That's why you were talking to Darren."

"I was hoping he had information for me, but there's nothing more he can tell me. If he knows where they are, he's good at hiding it."

Aubrey wouldn't be surprised if he did know something. Darren was a little shit, and Aubrey was sure he was hiding something. He probably thought he could use it as leverage to get out of the cell he was stuck in, but he was wrong. Oren would never let him leave, not when he and his little friends had been responsible for hurting Falkner and other vampires.

"I'll try talking to him," Falkner said. "Maybe he'll tell me something since I'm not you."

"I would be grateful, but I also don't expect much. He doesn't like talking to vampires," Oren answered.

Falkner smiled at him. "Then it's good I'm not a vampire." He looked at the door Oren had just come through. "I'll be back in half an hour. You'll be okay here, Aubrey?"

Aubrey beamed at him. "Of course. I'm not going anywhere."

Aubrey could swear he heard Oren mutter *unfortunately*. It made Aubrey smile, and he turned the beam toward Oren only to find that the man was already striding away.

Aubrey took a second to stare at his ass. Then he went after him.

Or at least, he tried to. His feet didn't seem to get the message, though, and he stumbled, falling on his face. He heard someone snicker, but he didn't even look. He was used to it.

Still. He might be used to it, but he *was* embarrassed, and he was pretty sure his nose was bleeding. He scrambled to get to his feet, then raised his hand to his face. It came back bloody, and he knew he needed to get away. He pressed his hand to his nose again, hoping to keep most of the blood there instead of getting his clothes soiled.

It was humiliating. He couldn't help it if he was a klutz, and becoming a vampire hadn't changed that. He'd learned to live with it, since he was a vampire and would technically live forever, but it didn't make it easier to accept.

"What happened?" Oren asked.

Aubrey jerked back. "Where did you come from?" His heart was racing. "I didn't hear you come back. You were leaving."

"And I came back when I heard you fall. Are you okay?" Oren asked again.

Aubrey grimaced and lowered his hand. "Let's just say I've been better. But don't worry. I know where the bathroom is." And Aubrey knew he could spend the entire time Falkner would be away in there. That way, people wouldn't stare at him. He might even be able to get over the embarrassment and come back to the entrance to look at the swords and paintings on the walls.

Oren shook his head. "You can't go to the bathroom."

"Where do you think I should go, then? I need to wash up."

Oren grunted, then grabbed Aubrey's wrist and pulled him closer as he started walking.

Aubrey's eyes widened when he realized where Oren was taking him. He'd never been there, but he knew the door they walked through led to the private quarters of the people who lived in the building, mostly conclave members and conclave teams. Maybe there was an infirmary there or something like that. Aubrey thought the infirmary was in another wing, but he didn't have a better explanation.

He was wrong. Oren stopped in front of a door and unlocked it, then pushed Aubrey inside. Aubrey realized it was Oren's bedroom as soon as he stepped foot inside, and he didn't know what to do with that. "I could just go to the infirmary," he suggested. "Or to the bathroom. I swear, I'm fine."

The only answer he got from Oren was a grunt. He looked around. He didn't want to get blood on anything, so he kept his hands close to his body.

The room looked like Oren in a way. Aubrey had expected it to be like this—serious, with not one personal object in sight. Neat, as if it wasn't even lived in. It was kind of sad, but it was Oren.

Aubrey rubbed the back of his neck, then realized his fingers were bloody. He jerked back, hoping he hadn't just spread his own blood all over his hair. "I'm sorry," he said. "I swear I won't get anything in here dirty, and if I do, I'll clean it up. And if I can't clean it, I'll buy you another one."

"Shut up." Oren didn't sound angry, and he wasn't snappish, so Aubrey knew that he wasn't saying it to be mean.

Aubrey swallowed. "You don't have to do this."

Oren came toward him, and he was holding a wet cloth.

"Sit down,"

Aubrey obeyed. There was a small table with a few chairs around it, and he sat in one of them, thinking that if he got them dirty, he could probably clean them easily. Oren went to work, using the cloth on Aubrey's face, and Aubrey didn't know what to say or do.

He'd never thought Oren would be the kind of man who was this caring. It didn't make sense, not when they barely knew each other. "I'm sorry for all of this," he said again. "I know I need to be more careful, but sometimes, my feet do whatever they want. I can't help it. I've tried, but I can't change it. But like I said before, I promise I'll clean everything." Oren moved the cloth away from Aubrey's face, and Aubrey winced at the sight of his blood on it. "I'll replace that, too. Don't worry."

Oren shook his head. Then, before Aubrey could realize what he was doing, he pressed their lips together.

Oren didn't think about what he was doing until his lips touched Aubrey's. He saw Aubrey's eyes widen, then his lips moved under Oren's, and Oren jerked back.

They stared at each other, and Oren was pretty sure his expression mirrored Aubrey's shock. He had no idea what he'd been thinking about.

He was pretty sure he hadn't been thinking, actually, not with his big head.

He'd always found Aubrey appealing. They didn't know each other well, but he'd seen Aubrey often enough. He was cute in an eager puppy kind of way. He was always bouncy, curious, and interested in just about everything, asking questions. His green eyes glittered with mirth and happiness, and Oren never wanted to take that away from him. Hell, he wanted to see it even more often. He wanted to be the reason

Aubrey was happy.

And that was impossible.

He cleared his throat and took a step back. "You're clean," he said gruffly.

Aubrey chuckled, the sound slightly hysterical. "And you know that because you were just licking my face."

"I wasn't licking your face," Oren said with a grunt.

"Those were your lips on mine, weren't they?"

Oren couldn't do this. He couldn't let Aubrey control the situation. He stood taller and took another step back. "I apologize for kissing you. I shouldn't have."

"Oh, you *should* have." Aubrey reached for him, and Oren knew he'd made a mistake when he allowed Aubrey to touch him. Aubrey pulled him closer until he could kiss him again, and Oren allowed him to.

He'd wanted this for a while. He'd wanted it since the first time he'd seen Aubrey, when Aubrey had dropped a sword to the floor in the entrance and everyone had looked at him. He'd wanted it when he'd seen how fiercely protective Aubrey was of his friends. He'd wanted it since the first time they'd talked and Aubrey had had so many questions that he'd made Oren's head hurt.

And he *still* wanted it.

But he shouldn't do it.

He was gentler this time when he stepped away from Aubrey. Aubrey blinked at him, his gaze slightly dazed, and Oren couldn't help but feel smug over the thought that he'd been the one to do that. Then, he remembered Lucas.

He couldn't do this again. His ex and he hadn't been together when he'd died, but he'd been killed by dhampirs, and dhampirs were in the city, killing vampires. What would Oren do if something happened to Aubrey? How would he react? He couldn't go through it a second time. He couldn't get close to Aubrey only to have him snatched away from him.

He had to focus on hunting the bad guys, not on getting a boyfriend. "I apologize again," he said, his voice stiff now.

Aubrey looked confused. "I don't," he finally said.

Oren was confused. "You don't what?"

"Apologize. For kissing you, I mean. I've wanted to do it for a while, and I'm happy you finally took the first step. I wasn't sure you liked me."

"It won't happen again," Oren said, the promise carrying in his voice.

Aubrey grimaced. "What if it did? Because I want to kiss you again. I want to kiss you, and to fuck you, and to have you fuck me."

Those words created images in Oren's brain, images he could have happily done without. Now he wasn't sure he would ever be able to avoid thinking about fucking Aubrey.

But he needed to be strong. Aubrey didn't understand why he couldn't be with him, and Oren didn't want to explain. Still, he needed Aubrey to know he wasn't playing around. "There can't be anything between us," he said, even though it was the last thing he wanted to say.

"Why not? We're both adults. I'm a vampire, so you don't have to worry about the conclave not being happy about it. I'm not going to turn into a werewolf while having sex or anything like that. I promise."

Oren shook his head. "I already know you're a vampire. It's not what I was talking about. We can't do this because of my job. I'm swamped with work, and you know how dangerous this job is. It wouldn't be fair."

For once, Aubrey didn't seem to have an answer. He stared at Oren, and Oren had to look away.

If he was honest with himself—and he tried to be—he wanted Aubrey. He wanted that kind of happiness and goofiness in his life. He sorely missed it, and he knew he was too serious, too stiff. People always told him he was boring, and he realized how true that was. Aubrey was anything but, though, and Oren desperately wanted to be close to him.

But he couldn't. Not only were his own chances of dying at the hands of a supernatural creature high, but with the dhampirs in town killing vampires, his chances of losing Aubrey were high, too.

"So you'll use work to keep me away," Aubrey said.

Oren frowned. "It's not an excuse. My job *is* dangerous. Do you want that kind of life? Do you want to wait every night when you know I'm out there hunting dhampirs and werewolves and wonder if I'll come home?"

Aubrey's eyes widened. "Well, I was thinking about sex, but you're not wrong. I do want to have a relationship with you."

Oren shook his head. "I just told you that's not possible." It was tempting to accept just having sex with Aubrey, but Oren wasn't an idiot. If they had sex, he would want more, and he wouldn't be able to resist for long. *No.* The only way for him to stay away from Aubrey was to keep his distance. That way, he wouldn't fall in love with him, and it would make his life easier.

Aubrey stepped closer. "I'm not that easily influenced or dissuaded," he said, his voice soft.

There was a strength in it that told Oren he was telling the truth. "There's nothing to dissuade you of. I told you there can be nothing between us, and I wasn't kidding."

"I'm not kidding, either. I want this, Oren. I want you, and the only reason I haven't done anything until now is that I wasn't sure you wanted me. Now I know you do."

"So, what—you'll force your way into my life?" Oren loathed his words, and he hadn't wanted to say them. They were too harsh, especially since he *did* want Aubrey in his life. He had to find a way to keep Aubrey away, though.

Aubrey arched a brow. "Would I be pushing my way into your life if you didn't want me? Probably not. But I *know* you want me. I don't care about the reasons you think you have not to give us this. They might be good reasons, but they don't matter, not when I want you and you want me. I'll get you to surrender, you'll see."

He was right. So far, Oren had viewed Aubrey as someone who took nothing seriously, but it was obvious that this, he was serious about. Oren was kind of afraid of what would happen next. Aubrey was stubborn, and he had set his sights on Oren.

He wouldn't stop until he got what he wanted, and the thought shouldn't have been as thrilling as it was.

Chapter Two

Babies shouldn't be as cute as Adrian was. Aubrey stared at him, wondering what he was supposed to do. He was babysitting, and Adrian was reaching for him to be taken into his arms. Aubrey wanted to obey the silent order, but Adrian had a tendency of throwing up on him when he did so. He didn't know why, and he didn't want to find out. He just knew that the baby liked to puke and poop when he was in his arms.

He wrinkled his nose. "What will you do if I hold you?" he asked. Adrian couldn't answer, but it didn't matter. It was a rhetorical question, anyway.

Aubrey sighed and reached for the baby. He gathered Adrian in his arms and smiled at him, and Adrian grabbed his nose. He pulled, but Aubrey wasn't even angry.

Then Adrian's expression twisted, and he grunted. Aubrey had known it would happen because it always did. He sighed, then headed toward the changing table. "Why do you do this to me?" he whined.

It made Adrian laugh. Aubrey couldn't help but smile.

It was hard to get distracted, though, even by Adrian. Aubrey's thoughts had been on Oren for days, and he doubted that would change soon. He had a hard time believing he and Oren had kissed, but he couldn't deny it. When he thought about it, he could still feel the tingling of Oren's lips on his, see the way Oren had stepped back, hear how he'd told him it had been a mistake.

Aubrey didn't think so. Kissing someone was rarely a mistake, but especially when two people cared for each other.

And he knew Oren cared.

Oren wouldn't have kissed him if he didn't. He wasn't that kind of man. Kissing Aubrey seemed to have been a spur-of-the-moment decision, and while Oren seemed to have regretted it, Aubrey didn't. He wanted more. Oren had taken care of him even though there had been no need for him to. Aubrey had fallen before, and he'd hurt himself before. He could have used the bathroom and gone on his way, and it wouldn't have changed anything for Oren. Instead, Oren had insisted. He'd brought Aubrey to his bedroom, and he'd taken care of him. He'd kissed him.

Then he'd freaked out.

Aubrey frowned as he changed Adrian's diaper. He didn't know Oren's past, but he suspected the way he behaved now had something to do with it. It was always the past, wasn't it? It was what made people behave the way they did. It was what influenced their decisions. Oren wasn't any different, and Aubrey was curious. Luckily for him, he knew who to ask, and when Ignatius came by to pick up Adrian after coming home from work, he was ready.

Ignatius smiled at Adrian, cooing over his son. The sight made something in Aubrey's chest squeeze almost painfully. He'd never thought about having children. Well, he hadn't thought about having children in a while. He had when he'd been human—when he'd thought he would marry a nice woman and have kids with her. Instead, he'd been turned into a vampire, and he'd lived that way since then. Being a vampire wasn't conducive to having children, although maybe he was wrong. Ignatius was a father now, and he seemed pretty happy about it. Adrian wasn't his son, not biologically, but it didn't seem to change anything for either of them or for Oscar, Ignatius' partner.

"How was he today?" Ignatius asked.

Aubrey bit his lower lip. "A pooping angel, like always. Do you have a moment?"

Ignatius frowned. "Is it about Adrian? Because you don't have to continue babysitting him if you'd rather not. I know you're uncomfortable with taking care of a baby, and we can find someone else."

"No. He's perfectly fine, and I'm okay with our arrangement." He hadn't been in the beginning. The first time he'd babysat, he'd done it because Ignatius and Oscar had been exhausted and needed rest. He'd had no idea what he was doing, and most days, he still didn't. He'd gotten used to dealing with a baby, though, and while he'd never enjoy changing Adrian, he was okay with everything else that came with the baby.

"Are you sure? Because if it's becoming a problem, I'm sure we can find someone else. I know you're busy protecting the coven, too."

Aubrey didn't want someone else to babysit Adrian. He might bitch about it, but he loved it. "Adrian is *not* a problem. I promise. I can continue babysitting him without a problem as long as it fits with the rest of my schedule."

Ignatius nodded. He looked confused, but he wasn't going anywhere, so Aubrey took that as a win. "Actually, I wanted to ask you about Oren."

Ignatius didn't look surprised. Aubrey doubted anyone in the house would be surprised at hearing that he wanted to find out more about Oren. Andrew, Falkner, and Richie had seen how Aubrey was with the man. They were always there when Aubrey went to the conclave building. Hell, the only reason he went was Falkner. That meant that they'd seen how chatty and clumsily stupid Aubrey became when Oren was around, and it hadn't taken him long to realize why that was. Falkner was more upfront, asking questions and giving advice, but Andrew and Richie were aware of the crush Aubrey had on Oren.

Now, so was Ignatius.

"What do you want to know about him?" Ignatius asked.

Aubrey had thought about this. He knew *exactly* what to

ask. "Did he lose someone?"

Ignatius blinked. "What do you mean?"

"I'm not sure. A boyfriend, a girlfriend, something like that?" Because it would make sense. Aubrey had thought Oren wasn't interested in him in the beginning, but now he knew the truth. Oren was, but something was stopping him from being with Aubrey, and Aubrey was planning on finding out what it was.

He was aware he could be wrong. Knowing Oren, it might just be that he wanted to focus on his job. Aubrey would ask Oren directly if he didn't think the man would hide away from him and avoid him. It was the kind of thing Oren would do. He'd use work as a shield, and something told Aubrey it wouldn't be the first time. So Aubrey was resorting to asking someone else. He wouldn't be angry if Ignatius didn't know or didn't tell him, though. He was aware this wasn't really his business.

"How did you know?" Ignatius asked.

So Aubrey was right. "I didn't know, not for sure. But something happened that made me think that was the case."

Ignatius slowly nodded. "He lost an ex-boyfriend. They weren't together when it happened, but it was horrible. Dhampirs got to him."

Aubrey grimaced. "And dhampirs are back in town."

"Exactly. Oren has been working himself to the bone since they arrived. He's not doing it consciously, but he feels guilty about what happened to his ex, even though he had nothing to do with it. None of us did. It was a surprise. No one was aware that dhampirs were in town back then. They're sneaky and are good at hiding and blitz attacks. It's how they're killing vampires right now. They know what they're doing and that we'll have a hell of a time finding and stopping them." Ignatius sighed. "I know you have something going on with Oren," he said.

Aubrey snorted. "Not really."

"Okay. I know you *want* something with Oren. I'm not sure it's going to happen, though, Aubrey. He's still hurting over the loss of his ex. Even though they weren't together, their breakup wasn't a bad one, and they still cared for each other. He's also very much focused on work."

Aubrey realized that, but now that he knew, he wasn't going to give up. He needed to come up with a plan, something that would show Oren he needed to give them a chance. He had to show Oren there was more to life than work. He understood Oren was still hurting over the loss of his ex and that his job was to protect the vampires in the city, which was hard to do with dhampirs on a killing spree. But there was more to life than loss and pain, and Oren would lose himself if he didn't take a step back from blood and death.

There was Aubrey, too. He wanted to be happy. He wanted *Oren* to be happy, even if it wasn't with him. He didn't know how he would manage to make that happen, but he would find a way.

Oren had to take better care of himself, and if he didn't, well, Aubrey would do it for him.

Oren looked around the crime scene. There wasn't much to see by now, but he wanted to make sure that if there was, he would notice.

It was yet another dead vampire, no doubt killed by dhampirs. These days, it seemed like all the vampires who died had been killed by the dhampirs. The problem was that they didn't exactly sign their crimes, so Oren couldn't be a hundred percent sure. He had to guess, and he didn't like doing that. He needed certainty. He needed to know what was happening, why it was happening, and how to solve it.

The vampire's head had been cut off. It was a standard way of killing a vampire, so really, it could have been anyone. Werewolves mauled vampires to death, so Oren was pretty sure he could take them out of the equation. But that still left way too many people and creatures who could have killed this vampire and all the ones that had come before him.

Oren rubbed his face. He'd already been over this crime scene several times since he'd arrived, and he still didn't have any more answers. Without knowing what the dhampirs were aiming for, it was hard for him to come up with a motive. Dhampirs would eventually become vampires if they had a violent death. Why would they want to kill the people they would become one day? Oren didn't understand, but then he supposed it made sense. He wasn't a dhampir.

Vampires viewed dhampirs with distaste at the very least, but most often, with disgust and hatred, and it was no doubt hard to be one. He might need to talk to Falkner to find out about that, but he wasn't looking forward to it. He knew Falkner was a dhampir because of the situation with Darren and that dhampir group, and that couldn't become common knowledge, for Falkner's sake. Besides, Falkner might be a dhampir, but most of all, he was a vampire—had been for a long time.

But Oren had to find the dhampirs and stop them. Even if they weren't behind this death, he knew for sure they'd killed other vampires. He couldn't allow this to continue. The *conclave* couldn't allow this to continue. They were there to protect vampires, to make sure nothing like this happened, and so far, they were failing. *Oren* was failing, and he didn't like it.

"I don't think we'll get anything else from the scene," Aline, one of his team members, said.

Oren nodded at her. "If we have everything, we can head back."

"I'll let everyone know."

Oren turned around and walked to their cars. He'd sent Ignatius home when he'd realize how late it was going to be. No matter how weird it was, Ignatius was a father now. He had more important things to do than sticking around crime scenes and trying to find proof of who had killed a vampire. He was still a conclave enforcer and a member of Oren's team, and that wouldn't change, but Oren realized his life had. He couldn't ask Ignatius to do what he'd done before, and even though he hadn't asked Ignatius yet, he was starting to wonder if maybe it wouldn't be a better idea to move Ignatius here permanently. Oren's team would eventually be sent away, and there was no way for them to know if or when they would be able to come back. Oren knew how important Ignatius' family was for him, and he was going to have to talk to him about it.

Not right now, though. Not when the only thing he could think about was stopping the dhampirs—and Aubrey. He had to stop him too, albeit in another way.

Oren shook his head. He had to forget about Aubrey. He had to focus on this and the other murders, on finding out whether the dhampirs had been behind it. For now, all he had about the string of murders was a hypothesis, and it wasn't enough. He needed to start thinking rationally, to find a way out of this, and that wouldn't happen until he knew for sure who the killers were.

Once he and the others got back to the conclave building, he sent them off to do their jobs. They'd worked several hours, gathering clues from the alley where they'd found the latest body, and it all had to be analyzed. Once he was sure they were all busy, Oren headed to the morgue.

The body had been transported there earlier, and the conclave medical examiner was already working on him. He wrinkled his nose but smiled at Oren when he saw him through the window. He waved, his gloved hand covered in blood, and Oren grimaced.

He might be used to it, but it didn't mean he was looking forward to this kind of stuff.

Caley came out after a while, still smiling. "I bet you want to know everything I have about the victim?"

"It's why I'm here, yes."

"You know it's too soon. I just came back with him. The only thing I can tell you for sure is that he was killed by decapitation."

Oren glared at him. "I could have told you the same thing. I saw him at the crime scene."

"You have to give me some time, Oren. I know how nervous you are about these cases, and I get it. Trust me. I don't like it, either, and I want this string of murders to end. But for that to happen, for me to give you any clues, I need time."

"We don't *have* time," Oren snapped. He took a deep breath. It wasn't Caley's fault that this was happening. He couldn't do anything more about it. He was already doing everything he could, as fast as he could.

Oren sighed. "I'm sorry," he said.

Caley blinked. "Sorry?"

"Yes. I know I've been pushing everyone hard. I apologize. I'll go away and give you time to do your job."

"I didn't think I'd ever see this in my life. You, apologizing."

Oren scowled. "I can apologize. I just did."

Caley waved him away. "Good. Keep that up, and you'll almost be a normal human being. Now shoo. I have work to do, and the sooner you leave, the sooner I can get back to it."

Oren obeyed, no matter how little he liked it. He wanted to push, to demand answers. He knew it didn't work like that, though. He left the area and went back to the main entrance, headed to his bedroom. It was only a few hours until sunrise, so he shouldn't stop working yet, but he was tired. He wasn't getting a lot of sleep lately, and it was as much because of the dhampirs as it was because of Aubrey.

Aubrey — who was currently standing in the middle of the entrance looking around like a lost puppy. His eyes widened when he saw Oren, and he beamed, making a beeline for him.

Oren contemplated his escape plan. He could try to ignore Aubrey and rush to his bedroom. He could act as if he hadn't seen him, which was tempting. He knew Aubrey wouldn't leave him alone, though. He never did.

"Oren!" Aubrey said when he reached Oren.

It was too late. Oren couldn't escape now. Instead, he crossed his arms over his chest and glared. "What are you doing here? Is Falkner talking to Darren again?"

"I'm here alone." And he sounded so damn proud of that. "I was wondering if you already ate dinner?"

Oren blinked. "I'm sorry?"

"Dinner. You know, the moment in which you sit down once the day is over and you eat before going to bed? Have you already eaten?"

"I haven't, but —"

Aubrey didn't even let Oren finish the sentence. To Oren's shock, he grabbed his hand and dragged him toward the exit. "Good. I took care of it, and I thought we could go outside and watch the sunrise."

Oren had no idea what to say to that. He wanted to refuse, mostly because he knew that whatever Aubrey had in mind, it didn't just include watching the sunrise and blood. He was here because of the kiss, well, of the kisses. He wanted to ask what was going on, or maybe he thought they were together now. Oren had no idea, and he didn't know how to deal with this.

He didn't want to hurt Aubrey. No matter how annoying

the vampire was, he was also endearing, and he was a good person. Excitable, always smiling, and annoying, but still a good person. Oren, on the other hand, wasn't. He felt awkward, especially once he and Aubrey left the building and sat outside, watching the sky become lighter.

Oren had half expected Aubrey to try to kiss him again, but instead, Aubrey limited himself to handing him a bottle of blood and turning toward the sky again. He was talking, although Oren wasn't sure about what. His brain didn't seem to be able to make sense of the words or the situation.

He didn't know what to do with Aubrey. He knew what he *wanted*, but it wasn't possible. Oren had decided a long time ago that he had to focus on his job, and the best way to do that was to avoid having a personal life.

Aubrey was babbling, and he didn't know how to stop. He'd always felt the need to fill silences, even when he'd been human, and spending time with Oren wasn't any different. Oren didn't talk. He was one of the quietest people Aubrey had ever known, and that meant that Aubrey's instinct was to talk even more than usual.

He hoped Oren liked talkative people. Aubrey supposed Oren would like them better if they were suspects and he was trying to solve a case, but luckily for Aubrey, he hadn't done anything wrong in a while. Well, unless one thought that dragging the man he had a crush on outside to watch the sunrise was wrong. He was pretty sure that was what Oren was thinking right now, but he happily ignored it.

He knew Oren was interested in him. He wasn't sure if the interest was just physical or if there was more to it, but he realized that more might mean complicated. He had no idea whether Oren was still in love with his ex-boyfriend or if the reason he was pushing Aubrey away was different. Maybe he just didn't like Aubrey's personality. He wouldn't be the first to feel that way, and even though it would hurt, Aubrey was aware that he couldn't expect everyone to like him. Some people hated him without reason. Some thought they had a good reason to hate him. It didn't matter.

He didn't want Oren to hate him, though. He hoped Oren didn't mind that he was talking too much. He hadn't said anything about it, but if Aubrey was honest, Oren looked a bit shellshocked. Aubrey didn't understand why, unless it was the talking. They both needed to have dinner, didn't they? So what if they did so together?"

Oren grunted, bringing Aubrey's attention back to him. Aubrey wanted more than what they had right now. He wanted to lean against Oren's side, to have Oren wrap his arm around him. He wanted them to enjoy the sunrise as a couple, to head to their bed after it was over, to spend the day together, to sleep and have sex.

Instead, Aubrey would go back to the coven on his own. He would go to bed on his own, and he would wake up still alone. His life had been the same for several decades, and he should be used to it by now. He supposed he was, but Oren was the possibility of more, and Aubrey wanted to take it.

Of course, Oren would have to be okay with that, and Aubrey still didn't know if that was the case.

So he talked. He wasn't even sure what he was talking about most of the time. He talked about the coven and its members. He told Oren about Fyfe and James, his werewolf boyfriend. He told him about Adrian, without mentioning the fact that Adrian was a vampire-werewolf hybrid. He was pretty sure Oren was aware of it, but just in case, he didn't want to reveal a secret that was best kept in the coven. They already had enough trouble with some of the coven members who didn't like that and wanted Adrian and Falkner to leave. They were bigots, all of them. Aubrey felt safe with the coven, but he realized that when people lived together, there were bound to be tensions and differences of opinion. Of course, thinking that dhampirs and other hybrids didn't have the right to live wasn't exactly a difference in opinion. It was bigotry, plain and simple, and Aubrey never hesitated to let the people he was talking to know what he thought about them if they were that kind of people.

He didn't think Oren was, though. Ignatius worked for him, and he'd told Aubrey that Oren was a good person. Falkner had been spending time with Oren every time he came to see Darren, and he thought the same thing. That meant that Aubrey was pretty sure Oren wouldn't have a problem with Adrian, but just in case, he needed to be sure before he said anything.

Once they were done eating, Aubrey got up. He could tell Oren expected him to do something, maybe to try to kiss him again, and he couldn't deny it was tempting. Oren *was* tempting, but Aubrey managed to stay away from him and behave as if he only felt friendship toward him. So far, it was all they were, and while it wasn't ideal, it was better than nothing.

"I'll walk you back inside," he said, taking the empty blood bottle from Oren's hands and putting it back into his backpack.

Oren frowned. "You don't have to walk me back."

Aubrey beamed at him. "I might not have to, but it doesn't mean I don't want to. Come on."

Oren shook his head, but to Aubrey's relief, he got up and followed Aubrey inside.

Aubrey wasn't sure he'd obtained anything tonight. He'd wanted to take care of Oren, to show him that he cared. He suspected Oren didn't take much time to sit down and eat every day, and he wanted that to change. He knew better than to hope it would, but he might be able to help at least a little bit. He could make sure Oren had food, that he ate regularly, and that he took some time to breathe every day. The kind of job he had, investigating horrible deaths, hunting people, couldn't be easy, even if those people deserved it. Everyone needed a break sometimes, but Oren didn't seem like the kind of person who allowed himself to pause.

Aubrey was going to make sure that changed, whether or not they ended up together.

"Will you go to bed now?" he asked as he and Oren walked back into the entrance. It was still busy, even though dawn was coming.

"Of course not. I still have work to do," Oren said.

Aubrey rolled his eyes. "You do know that the work will still be there this evening, right?"

"I need to solve this as soon as possible. People are dying, Aubrey. It's not a game, and I can't afford to waste time."

Aubrey wanted to yell at Oren that he knew that, but he doubted yelling at Oren would achieve anything, so instead, he shook his head. "I know. But working yourself to death isn't going to help anyone. You might be strong, but you're still human, just like all of us. You need blood and sleep. You need companionship. Not allowing yourself to have that is going to impact your work negatively, and I know it's the last thing you want."

Oren blinked at him. "I don't know what to do with you," he confessed, looking like he regretted it as soon as words were out.

Aubrey beamed at him. "Don't worry. You have time to figure it out."

He ignored Oren's grumbling and walked him back to the door that led to the private quarters. He didn't know if Oren would listen to him and go to bed, but he doubted it. Besides, it wasn't that late yet. He wanted more time with Oren, but he had to go home before the sun was entirely out. It was going to be painful as it was, and he couldn't risk it.

"I should go," he said.

Oren frowned. "Will you be able to? With the sun, I mean?"

"Don't worry about me. I'll be fine."

Oren hesitated. "You're sure? I can get someone to drive you back to the coven."

He was worried. That meant he cared, right? Aubrey didn't know, but he wanted to hope.

He nodded. "I'm sure." Acting on a whim, he leaned closer and quickly kissed the corner of Oren's lips. "I'll see you soon," he said, promise in his voice.

Oren looked like he wasn't sure how to take it, and Aubrey didn't give him time to protest. He turned around and headed to the door, knowing he had to be quick.

It had been a risk, both physically because he might get sunburned, and emotionally because Oren could have rejected him. Instead, Oren had had dinner with him, even if it was a picnic outside and he hadn't said more than a few words. Not exactly the perfect first date, but it was a step forward, and it was more than Aubrey had allowed himself to hope for.

Oren didn't know what had just happened. He watched Aubrey walk away, wondering what this was all about.

Aubrey always surprised him. The first time he'd met him, Aubrey had given him the impression that he was a protector. Then he'd dumped a sword on the floor, and Oren had thought he was a mess. That opinion only lasted a few moments, though. He'd seen how much Aubrey cared for his friends right from the beginning. He'd seen the way Aubrey made sure Falkner was okay and safe and that nothing would happen to him when they came around to talk to Darren. It was endearing, and now that they'd spoken a few times, Oren knew there was more to Aubrey than Aubrey let people see.

Which was why he was sure that whatever had just happened, whatever Aubrey had in mind with this dinner, there was more to it than Oren had been able to read. He wanted to take his time thinking about this, but he couldn't. He couldn't put his heart or Aubrey's at risk, and that was what would happen if he gave this—whatever *this* was—a chance.

He wanted to. He was tired of being alone, of pushing everyone away, of waking up alone. But even if the dhampirs hadn't been in town right now, even if the situation didn't remind Oren of when he'd lost Lucas, Oren wouldn't be able to do this. He wouldn't stay in the city forever. Eventually, once the dhampirs were dealt with, his team would be sent away. It was the life of the conclave teams. They were sent where they were needed, and they could spend a long time away from home, working on cases, driving around the country. That meant he would have to leave Aubrey behind, and he couldn't ask that of him. Aubrey needed someone who could be with him, who could support him and love him from close by, not from afar. He needed someone who would make him his priority, while Oren's priority would always be work. It had always been work, even before Lucas' death. It was the reason they'd broken up, and the reason Lucas had been alone that night.

Oren shook his head, eyed the door that would lead him to his bedroom, then turned away. He might just have had dinner, but he was too keyed up to go to bed. His thoughts wouldn't stop swirling, going back and forth between the murders, the dhampirs, and Aubrey. Oren never allowed them to stop for long on Aubrey, but he couldn't deny that the other vampire filled his mind.

Oren wanted to find out where this would go. He wanted to find out if he and Aubrey were compatible and if they could have something. For that to happen, though, Oren would have to allow himself to be vulnerable. He would have to put Aubrey in danger, to put him in the path of the dhampirs. He would have to hurt him, to make him sad.

That was why it would never happen.

He headed to the cafeteria. There wasn't food there, since vampires didn't eat, but the wide fridges along the wall were filled with bottles of blood. He ignored them, sitting at one of the tables in the corner instead, then taking his phone out to go over his notes. He wouldn't be able to sleep, but he could work.

He wasn't sure how long he'd been sitting there when the chair on the other side of the table moved back. He jerked, glaring at Caley, who sat in front of him, holding an open bottle of blood with both his hands. Oren could smell it, and it made his stomach grumble. "What are you doing here? Shouldn't you be working on the autopsy?" he asked.

Caley glared at him. "I'm going back soon, don't worry. I'm allowed a break, though, aren't I?"

Oren grimaced. Sometimes, he forgot how to be human. He forgot that not everyone focused on work as much as he did. "Of course you are. Sorry."

Caley shook his head. "Don't apologize for being yourself. Don't worry about it."

"Of course I worry about it. I don't want to be a dick."

Caley laughed. "It's too late for that. You're a dick most of the time. But that's okay. I know that, and I love you anyway."

Oren couldn't help but smile. He might not spend a lot of time in town, but he and Caley had been friends for what felt like forever, and he loved him, too.

Caley tapped his fingertips on the table. "I have something for you," he finally said.

That got Oren's attention, and he straightened in his seat. "What?"

"I just got the results for the last two bodies."

"The blood tests?" That was the only thing they were still waiting for. Caley had already examined the other bodies, and there wasn't much to say about them. They'd been decapitated, just like tonight's victim. That was all he'd had been able to say, and it was one of the reasons Oren had no idea what to do next. The bodies hadn't given him anything, no clues, no proof.

Caley nodded. "Those. They came back positive for a sedative usually used on horses."

"A sedative?" Oren frowned. "How, though? They were all killed in isolated alleys and streets. How could someone have sedated them?"

Caley shrugged. "Well, their stomach contents showed that they had eaten shortly before being killed."

Oren's frown deepened. "You mean they were given tainted blood? That someone drugged them through that?"

Caley looked around, then leaned closer. "Do you want to know what I think happened, or do you want me to stick to the proof I have?"

Oren hesitated. He knew he should ask for Caley's opinion. His friend was a medical examiner, not an enforcer. He didn't have experience with investigative work. Still, he knew the bodies better than anyone. "Tell me what you think."

Caley nodded. "I think they were drugged, yes. I think that someone allowed themselves to be bitten and that they had taken the sedative beforehand."

"So you think the vampires were drugged through the blood of the person they bit." It made sense. Dhampirs were human, after all. A vampire wouldn't notice the difference between their blood and a normal human being. If they were enticing enough, or if the vampire wasn't scrupulous enough, it would be entirely possible for them to be drugged that way.

"I do. It makes sense. I can't give you proof of that,

though."

Oren rubbed his face. "This is a mess," he muttered.

"That, it is. I already told the lab technicians I want the blood of this last victim examined immediately. I hope I'll have news for you by tomorrow, but I'm not making any promises."

"Thank you. This is more than enough." It was, yet at the same time, it wasn't. Because even though now they knew how dhampirs managed to kill the vampires, it still wouldn't help Oren find them.

"I heard something interesting," Caley said.

"About the dhampirs?"

Caley shook his head. "About your boyfriend."

It took Oren a second to realize who he was talking about, and when he did, he scowled at his friend. "He's not my boyfriend."

"Not yet, maybe. But eventually. I heard he came by tonight to see you. That you left with him and didn't come back for a while."

Sometimes Oren couldn't stand living here. The conclave was a serious organization, and the people who worked for them should be just as serious. Instead, they acted like a bunch of gossipy ladies. Oren knew better than to ask Caley who had told him that, though. Caley wouldn't tell him, not when he knew Oren was angry. "We had dinner together. That's all."

"I'm just saying it was about time," Caley said, raising his hands.

"He's not my boyfriend, and he'll never be my boyfriend," Oren said. "You know it's not possible."

"I know *you* don't think it's possible," Caley answered, arching a brow. "That's your opinion. I doubt Aubrey shares it."

"You know about my past, about Lucas. I can't do this,

especially not with dhampirs in town. What if Aubrey is attacked? What if I'm too distracted to help him or other victims? I can't be distracted."

"You're only human, Oren. No matter how much you dislike it, you can't deny it. It means that you get tired, hungry, and yes, distracted. No one expects you not to have a personal life, even while dealing with this. Give yourself a break. Give Aubrey a chance."

Oren wanted to do that desperately, but he couldn't. It didn't matter what Aubrey and Caley thought. Oren had to focus on his job. He had to save the dhampirs' next victims, and that wouldn't happen if he couldn't stop thinking about Aubrey.

Chapter Three

Aubrey was bouncing on the balls of his feet when he arrived at the conclave building a few days after his dinner with Oren. He'd wanted to come back sooner, but he didn't want to push Oren too much. He realized it was a good thing that Oren had agreed to have dinner with him without a protest. He couldn't push his luck yet, though. Besides, life had happened, and he'd been busy with Adrian and his job.

He missed Oren. He couldn't deny his end goal was to have a relationship with him, but of course, that wouldn't happen until Oren was okay with it. If he never was, well, Aubrey would have gained a friend. Still, he suspected Oren felt the same way about him as he felt about Oren, and he had hope. He needed to be careful and not to push too hard, too fast, but he could do that.

Maybe. *Hopefully.*

Aubrey wasn't exactly a patient man, but Oren would be worth it. Aubrey already knew that.

So he was back again, alone because Falkner wasn't planning on seeing Darren today, and he hoped Oren would give him at least a half-hour of his time. Maybe they could have lunch or dinner together or something. At this point, Aubrey would take anything Oren offered him.

He pushed open the door, and the guard at the entrance looked up. She rolled her eyes, used to seeing Aubrey there by now, and pointed toward the back of the wide entrance. Aubrey wasn't sure where all the doors led yet. He'd been in Oren's private room and the interrogation rooms, but he didn't know about the other doors. The one the guard was pointing at was one of those, and Aubrey was giddy to find out what was behind it. He strode toward it, but before he could get there, it opened, and Oren stepped out.

Aubrey huffed. He was curious about what was going on be behind all those closed doors, dammit.

Oren noticed him, and his eyes widened slightly. Then his expression shuttered, and he came toward Aubrey. He was tense, and Aubrey suspected something had happened. He wasn't surprised when Oren came to stand in front of him and looked down at him, asking, "What are you doing here?"

Aubrey beamed at him. "I wanted to see you."

"Do you know how dangerous it is?"

Aubrey frowned. "I'm not sure what you're talking about."

Oren looked around. They were attracting attention, and Aubrey knew Oren didn't like that. He wasn't surprised when Oren gestured toward the door that would lead them to Oren's bedroom, but he *was* surprised when Oren took his wrist and dragged him toward it. Maybe he wasn't quick enough for Oren's taste. Whatever the case, Aubrey didn't mind. He liked having Oren's hands on his body, even if it was only his wrist.

Oren was uncomfortably silent until they reached his bedroom. He dragged Aubrey inside. Then he closed the door behind them and turned to look at him. "Don't you know how dangerous it is out there?" he repeated.

Aubrey sat on the edge of the mattress. Oren hadn't told him he could, but if they were having any kind of conversation—and it looked like they were—he wanted to be comfortable. "You're going to have to give me more details," he said. "What's going on?"

Oren moved in front of Aubrey. "What's going on? Are you telling me you don't know about the dhampirs? Because one of your friends visits one of them regularly."

Aubrey blinked. "I know about dhampirs. I know they're still in town. I don't see what the problem is."

"The problem? You've been running around the city on your own. That's exactly how the dhampirs find their victims.

They target lone vampires, and they attack them and decapitate them. Do you really want to end that way?"

Aubrey understood now. Oren was afraid.

He shouldn't be surprised. He knew about Oren's ex-boyfriend, who had been killed by dhampirs. Even if Oren didn't feel anything more than friendship for Aubrey, he was obviously afraid that Aubrey would meet the same end. It made something in Aubrey's chest soften. He still didn't know if Oren cared for him the way he cared for Oren, but it was an indication that he did.

As were the kisses they'd shared.

He rose to his feet. He needed to be careful about what he said. He didn't want to make Oren angry, or rather, angrier than he already was. He also didn't want Oren to see him like a useless and defenseless person, though. "You do know that I'm one of the enforcers for the coven, don't you?" he asked.

Oren looked at him like he couldn't comprehend his words. "I do."

"That means I'm trained. I train every day. I know I look and sound like an idiot most of the time, but I wouldn't be in charge of the coven security if Fyfe didn't trust me with it. I know what I'm doing, Oren. I might not work for the conclave, but it doesn't mean I'm not good at my job."

Oren raked a hand through his hair. "You don't understand. The dhampirs are dangerous. They've been killing people left and right, and I have no idea how to stop them. Hell, I don't even know for sure that *they* are the ones behind all the murders."

"You don't?"

Oren shook his head. "I strongly suspect them, but they never leave any proof behind. I have no way to be sure, no matter how much I want to. I also have no way to find out where they are. I don't want you to go around on your own, Aubrey. You or any of your friends. It's too dangerous."

Aubrey was touched by Oren's concern, but he couldn't let this go. Even though he wanted Oren to care about him and to worry about his safety, he didn't want Oren to order him around.

He stepped closer and put himself in front of Oren, making sure the man was looking at him. "You're not my keeper," he said, keeping his voice gentle. "You're also not my boyfriend. You can't tell me what to do."

Oren looked like Aubrey had kicked him in the nuts. He sputtered, then pointed his finger at Aubrey. "I don't care that I'm not your keeper or your boyfriend. I'm a conclave enforcer, and you have to listen to me. I give orders, and you follow them."

Aubrey was both irritated and amused. "You can try to force me to follow your rules, sure. The last time I checked, though, the conclave can't force vampires to do anything. They don't have a say in how I live my life. The only reason the conclave was created was to keep vampires under control, to protect them, and to make sure none of us outs us to the humans. You're good at your job, but telling me what to do isn't a part of it."

Aubrey could see Oren was angry, and he understood it. Oren wanted him to be safe, just like he wanted Oren to be safe. If he had a choice, he would wrap Oren in cotton and keep him away from all dangers of life. He certainly wouldn't allow him to run around the city hunting dhampirs.

But he *didn't* have a say in it. He couldn't tell Oren what to do or what not to do. It wasn't his place, just like it wasn't Oren's place to do the same with him.

He sighed. "Look," he started, unsure how to continue. "You're worried. I get it. I'm a pretty lovable person, and you're starting to care about me." Oren opened his mouth, no doubt to protest and tell Aubrey to fuck off, but Aubrey shook his head and continued. "And I might look like a goof. I'm clumsy. But I do know how to protect myself, and how to protect the coven. I won't allow you to tell me what to do with my life unless you have a good reason for that."

Oren cocked his head to the side. "And being your boyfriend would be a good reason?"

Aubrey beamed at him. "It would be a *perfect* reason. If my boyfriend were to tell me that he was worried about me and how much time I spend away from the coven, I would take what he thinks into consideration."

"What about a man who likes you? Someone who might fall in love with you eventually?"

Aubrey's heart raced. He couldn't believe he was here, having this conversation with Oren. "I'll consider that, too. As long as that man knows that telling me he likes me means I'm going to expect him to at least try to be in a relationship with me."

Oren looked like he was about to say no. Instead, he sucked in a breath, then nodded curtly. "Okay. I have feelings for you, Aubrey. I don't know what they are, and I don't want to analyze them right now. I just need you to promise me that you're going to be careful and stay home."

This wasn't exactly how Aubrey had imagined the moment would go, but he supposed he couldn't be picky, not when Oren had told him he could fall in love with him—eventually.

Oren didn't like having to do this. Aubrey had pushed him into it, and he didn't want to do it. He had to, though. It was obvious Aubrey knew what he was doing. He thought he'd won. Maybe he had. Aubrey had been pushing and pulling for Oren to admit that he felt something for him, and Oren couldn't say no, not when Aubrey's safety was in jeopardy.

"There. Now you know how I feel about you," he said, looking away.

"You could look less like it was painful to admit that," Aubrey pointed out.

Oren glared at him. "I can't, because it *was* painful. You were never supposed to find out. You weren't supposed to become part of my life." He didn't want to admit it, either to himself or to Aubrey. It had been easier to ignore the feelings he had for him than to deal with them when he hadn't acknowledged them. But now he had, and he would never be able to deny them. Aubrey knew, and so did he.

Aubrey stepped closer. "I know you're worried," he murmured. "I know why you don't want me to come here or to leave the coven on my own. I get it. It's your job to protect people, and you have feelings for me, so of course, you want to protect me. Don't you see that I want to protect you, too? I want you to be safe. I don't want you to hunt dhampirs and to get yourself killed before we can have anything. The thought of that happening to you is terrifying, but I would never ask you not to do this. It's your job, your life, and I have no say in it."

Oren swallowed. It had been a long time since someone had cared about him this way. He knew his team members cared, of course, and so did the few friends he had, like Caley.

Aubrey was different, though. The last person Oren had allowed in his life this way had been Lucas, and Lucas had died. He'd cared, though. He, too, had wanted Oren to be happy and safe. He'd done everything he could to make that happen, and Oren had pushed him away. He should do the same thing with Aubrey. He should make sure Aubrey stayed away from him and went his own way. He shouldn't allow himself to give in, to hope.

But even though he knew that, and even though he was aware of it, he still leaned forward and kissed Aubrey.

Aubrey made a surprised sound, but he leaned against Oren. His arms slipped around Oren's waist, wrapping around him and holding him close.

Oren didn't protest. He yearned to be close to Aubrey. He wanted to kiss him like there was no tomorrow, to have him at least for one moment. He knew it wouldn't last long. It couldn't, not when he had to focus on the job, not when he'd already lost one man to it. But maybe he could have this.

It wouldn't be easy to get Aubrey to leave him alone afterward, but for once, Oren didn't want to think about the consequences. He didn't want to think about what would happen next. He wanted Aubrey, and Aubrey wanted him. Shouldn't that be enough at least for half an hour?

He grabbed Aubrey and hauled him closer. Aubrey squeaked and laughed, but Oren shut off the sounds with his mouth. He sucked on Aubrey's bottom lip, wanting to be even closer, to go deeper. He wanted to be part of Aubrey's body, and this was the only way he knew how to do it.

He pushed Aubrey to the bed. Aubrey went without a protest, without trying to stop him. He was strong enough to push Oren away or to tell him that he didn't want something, so Oren didn't worry about that. Instead, he worried about taking Aubrey's pants off his body.

Aubrey laughed and gave him a hand. He unbuttoned his jeans and pushed them down his long legs, then reached for his t-shirt. Since Aubrey had everything in hand, Oren took care of his own clothes, dumping them in a pile on the floor and climbing onto the bed. Aubrey was still tangled in his t-shirt, and while Oren could have helped him, he decided he had better things to do. He sucked a hickey next to Aubrey's belly button, making Aubrey groan and wiggle under him.

"It's not fair. I can't get rid of this," Aubrey whined from under the t-shirt.

Oren kissed a path up, stopping when he reached Aubrey's covered face. Then he helped Aubrey take off the t-shirt and threw it away. They were face to face, both naked, Aubrey's body warm against Oren's.

Oren kissed him again. Aubrey made a satisfied sound, almost like a cat purring, and Oren nearly lost it. He'd wanted this for so long, ever since he'd first seen Aubrey. He knew he shouldn't be doing it, but he couldn't have stopped himself even if he'd wanted to.

And he definitely didn't.

Instead, he wanted to open Aubrey up for himself, to sink into him and make him his. He wanted to possess him, for them to be each other's everything.

He had to stop. It was a dangerous kind of thinking, and he needed to focus on the fact that this could only be sex. He might have just admitted to Aubrey that he was falling in love with him, but he *could* stop it. He could stop himself from having more feelings for the man.

Or at least, he hoped he could.

As he kissed Aubrey, he ran his hands along Aubrey's body. Aubrey made everything easy for him, opening his legs and allowing him to slot his body between them. They fit together perfectly, no matter how corny it sounded. It was as if Aubrey had been made for Oren, and Oren wished he had been. He wished vampires could have soulmates just like in the books and the movies, even though it was a ridiculous thought. But he wanted something to bind him to Aubrey — to make Aubrey his. He knew he just had to say the words and it would happen, but he couldn't. He had to keep himself in check before things went too far.

So he focused on Aubrey's body. That was the easiest thing to do, mostly because *Aubrey* made it easy. He allowed Oren to touch him anywhere Oren wanted. He groaned and moaned and whimpered as Oren played with his body, touching every single inch he could reach. He left bite marks on Aubrey's neck, his chest, his stomach. He sucked hickeys on the inside of his thighs. He never touched Aubrey's cock, no matter how much he and Aubrey both wanted him to.

Oren wanted more. The thought terrified him, even as the feelings seeped in every single touch that he gave Aubrey's body.

He knew Aubrey could feel this was more than sex. He knew Aubrey could feel the love already felt for him every time he touched and kissed him. He wanted to deny it, to tell Aubrey not to hope for anything more, to tell him it was only sex and that he didn't feel anything for him. It would be a lie, though, and they would both know it—he'd already said it. He could ignore that, but it wouldn't make the words fade or take them back.

"You're driving me crazy," Aubrey murmured.

Oren was driving himself crazy, and he needed to slow down. He didn't want to, though. He kissed Aubrey harder and settled between his legs again, allowing Aubrey to hold him. They rutted against each other, and Oren had to resist the urge to mark Aubrey, to make him his, to bite his neck and draw blood to show the entire world Aubrey was taken. Oren wasn't an animal, but he sure felt like one as they brought each other to completion.

It was frantic and sweaty and painful, because he knew what had to happen next. He knew he would have to let Aubrey go once it was over, and that loss tarnished every single touch they exchanged. It tainted their release, the moment they slumped to the mattress, still pressed together, holding each other like lovers. He wanted to continue. He wanted to give himself a moment to enjoy this because he knew it wouldn't happen again anytime soon. It was wrong, but he was only human after all, so instead of pushing away from the bed and from Aubrey as soon as he'd come, he closed his eyes and sucked in a breath.

Aubrey felt Oren relax, and for one moment, he allowed himself to think that this was it. Oren had accepted how he felt for Aubrey, and what they'd just done was the first step toward a relationship.

He knew better than to hope, though. He knew that eventually — *soon* — Oren would think about what he was doing, and he would get up. He would close himself off, and he would kick Aubrey out.

Aubrey wasn't surprised when Oren did exactly that. He tried to hold onto the man, to make the moment last for a bit longer, but after a few minutes, Oren pushed himself off the bed — and off Aubrey. He didn't look Aubrey in the face, and Aubrey sighed.

Oren's reaction wasn't unexpected, but that didn't mean Aubrey had to simply take it. He wanted a relationship with Oren. He'd been clear about that, and for a moment, he'd allowed himself to hope. Oren had told him he had feelings for him. He'd thought this was it, that it was the beginning of their relationship.

But Oren wasn't like that. He was dedicated to his cause, and right now, he thought that cause dictated to him that he couldn't have a personal life — that he couldn't have a boyfriend, someone to come home to at night. Aubrey wasn't ready to accept defeat yet, but he knew he couldn't push, not now. Oren needed some space to think and to deal with what they'd just done. Maybe it would help. Maybe it wouldn't. Aubrey had no way to know, and he wasn't going to find out now.

He pushed himself off the bed and looked around for his clothes. His t-shirt was close by, so he grabbed it and put it on, wincing when he realized his body was still sticky with sweat and their combined releases.

"You don't have to go," Oren said.

Aubrey jerked his focus toward him. The big man wasn't

looking at him, and he was rubbing the back of his neck and looking awkward. Aubrey couldn't help but wonder if he meant what he'd said. Probably. He might want Aubrey to stay because he knew it was what Aubrey wanted, and it was tempting to say yes and to get back into bed, to take off his t-shirt and bask in the memories of what they'd just done.

But Aubrey could tell Oren was uncomfortable. He wasn't sure *what* Oren was uncomfortable with, so he continued dressing, but instead of rushing out the door the way he'd planned to, he sat on the mattress again. He waited, wondering what Oren was thinking, what he wanted.

When Oren still didn't say anything and just stood there, naked, Aubrey gave him a crooked grin. "I can't say I'm not enjoying the view, but I'm pretty sure you would be more comfortable if you were dressed." After all, this was the first time they'd been naked together. Oren had nothing to be ashamed of when it came to his body, but Aubrey understood that not everyone was comfortable with nudity.

Oren's cheeks flushed, something Aubrey hadn't thought possible. It was adorable, and it made him look like a big teddy bear. He *was* a big teddy bear, at least when it came to some things. Aubrey had no doubt that Oren was lethal when he wanted to be, which was most of the time, but he loved seeing the small signs of vulnerability, of the man under the shield Oren always kept up.

Oren slipped back into his underwear.

Aubrey took his hand and brought him close, then He rose to his feet and kissed Oren again, sighing against his lips.

He wanted more. He wanted to be able to stay the night, to drag Oren back to the coven. He wanted to tell Oren that they could do this, that they were perfect for each other. He wanted to be here in bed when Oren came home after work, tired and needing to talk about something that wasn't death and trouble.

He couldn't have any of that, though. He didn't know if he ever would, but he kissed Oren, making sure Oren would miss him once he was gone. He wanted Oren to remember this moment, for it to be just as important to him as it had been to Aubrey.

Aubrey stepped away when they were both out of breath. He could feel Oren's cock hardening against him again, and while he wanted nothing more than to get back in bed and go at it a second time, he had to go.

He cleared his throat. "I had fun," he said.

Oren snorted. "Of course you did."

"I hope we can do this again." Aubrey prayed they would. He knew it would be touch and go for a while, though. Oren would have to admit that he wanted this and that he hopefully wanted more than sex. Aubrey wasn't holding his breath just yet, though.

He stepped closer again and kissed Oren's cheek. "I care for you," he admitted. "I'm half in love with you already, and I doubt that will change anytime soon. Well, if it does, it's going to be for the worst, from your point of view. Because you're a lovable man, Oren, and I want nothing more than to be allowed to love you. But I understand that you don't want that, and that's okay. We can do just sex for now if it's the only thing you're comfortable with."

Oren frowned. "You only want to have sex with me?"

"Of course not. I want everything with you. I want us to fall in love and to have a life together." Aubrey realized it was probably too much, too soon, but Oren already knew how he felt. He'd made it obvious, and even though the words were scary, they were nothing new. "But I understand that you might not be ready for this, or that you might not want it." Aubrey hesitated. He didn't want Ignatius to get in trouble, but maybe Oren should know he was aware of his ex. "I know you lost someone to dhampirs." Oren opened his mouth, but

Aubrey shook his head. "You don't have to say anything. I wasn't given any details, but I do know you lost him, and I understand why this situation is scary for you. There are dhampirs in town, and I'm going around on my own. I'm not a child, though. I know what I'm doing, and I can defend myself. I'm not going to hide. I won't stop living my life just because I could meet a dhampir. You shouldn't worry about me."

Oren snorted. "That's not going to be possible."

Aubrey couldn't help but smile. "I know. But I'll be as careful as I can. You're going to have to trust me on that." He kissed Oren again, sweet and gentle this time. "Can I see you again, then? Only for sex, if that's the only thing you're comfortable with." Aubrey knew himself well enough to be aware that he wouldn't be able to do the *only sex* thing for any length of time. Hell, even what they'd just done wasn't only sex. He was already in love with Oren. Having sex with him would only make that worse, but he was ready to take the risk.

He'd gotten his heart broken more than once over his long life. He could take it again.

He didn't wait for Oren to give him an answer, no matter how much he wanted to. Oren had his phone number, and he knew where to find him if he wanted to, so after one last kiss—it always seemed to be the last one, yet Aubrey couldn't resist kissing Oren again—Aubrey stepped back. If he didn't leave, he never would. "I'll see you around," he told Oren. "Call me if you want to."

Then Aubrey turned around and headed toward the door.

His entire being was pushing at him to stay, to climb into Oren's lap and stay there forever. Instead, he never looked behind as he left Oren's bedroom and walked down the hallway. He was pretty sure everyone could tell what he'd just done, and he didn't care. Some of the hickeys Oren had sucked on his body were probably visible from under the collar of his t-shirt, but he bore them as marks he was proud of. Oren had left them on him. They were a sign of what they'd done, and hopefully, of what they would do again soon.

Aubrey knew his heart would be broken if Oren decided he never wanted to see him again, but he'd deal with that when the time came.

Hopefully, it never would.

The door had already closed behind Aubrey, but Oren couldn't look away. He couldn't believe what he'd just done. Aubrey had told him he was in love with him, that he cared about him and that he wanted more, and how had Oren answered? He hadn't said anything, and instead, he'd basically kicked Aubrey out right after they'd had sex. They hadn't even cuddled, for fuck's sake, and cuddles were the best part of sex.

Oren groaned and rubbed his face with both his hands. Aubrey made him feel awkward, and he didn't like it. He wasn't awkward. He always knew what he wanted, and he did everything he could to get it. It was different with Aubrey, though. It was as if he'd released a part of Oren that was always hidden, and Oren didn't know how to deal with it. He didn't know how to be vulnerable with someone. His first instinct was to close himself off, not to allow Aubrey in, and he knew that was what he should do. Why didn't he want to, then?

He was an asshole. He wanted to do what Aubrey wanted — give to in to the feelings he knew they shared. He wanted to be with Aubrey, but he was terrified.

He liked Aubrey too much. Hell, he was falling in love with him. That meant losing him would hurt just like losing Lucas had, and Oren didn't know if he could face that again.

He and Lucas had broken up before his death because of Oren's job. Lucas hadn't wanted him to continue working for the conclave. He'd been afraid something would happen to Oren, and they'd constantly fought about it, especially with dhampirs in town. Lucas had had enough, and he'd told Oren not to come back if he didn't quit his job.

Oren hadn't quit. He'd packed his bag and moved into the conclave building of the city they were living in back then, and that was the last time he'd seen Lucas alive. He didn't even know if they'd officially broken up when Lucas was killed, and he didn't think it mattered. He hadn't been there for Lucas. He had loved him, but loving him hadn't been enough. What if the same happened with Audrey? Aubrey seemed to understand better than Lucas that Oren needed to do his job, but maybe it was just a façade. Maybe it would change if they were together, and Aubrey would demand that Oren quit his job, too.

Oren couldn't, and he didn't want to. He liked protecting people. He liked the responsibility that went with it. He loathed finding bodies and having to investigate murders, having to punish people who had done bad things, but it was necessary. He and the other conclave enforcers kept the entire vampire species safe and made sure humans didn't find out about them. It was Oren's job, and he liked doing it.

He also liked Aubrey, though.

He huffed and headed to the bathroom. He wanted more time with Aubrey, but since he wouldn't have it, he could go back to work. It had been a nice break, but he couldn't forget that people were dying out there. He had to stop the dhampirs, and to do that, he needed to find where they were. It was next to impossible, but Oren wasn't easily dissuaded. He was a fighter, and he would find a way.

He quickly showered, then dressed and headed out. His

thoughts were still twirling around Aubrey, so he decided he should go to the gym. Maybe training for a while would help him push Aubrey out of his thoughts. He didn't want that to happen, but it had to. Until and unless the dhampir problem was taken care of, Oren couldn't allow himself to focus on anything else, least of all Aubrey.

He stepped into the gym and almost turned around to head back to his bedroom. One of his team members, Robin, was there, running on one of the treadmills. He looked up and waved at Oren, and Oren sighed and waved back. He stepped onto the treadmill next to Robin's, glad that Robin wasn't one of the talkative members of his team.

"What's up?" Robin asked.

Oren contemplated not answering, but even though his team members knew he was gruff and quiet, Robin would know something was up if Oren ignored him entirely. Still, Oren wasn't about to confess what had just happened or to talk about his feelings. "I'm worried," he admitted.

Robin nodded. "About the murders. We all are."

"Yeah. I hate that we still don't know where the dhampirs are. We need to flush them out, but how?"

This was easy. It was what Oren knew and what he needed. Even though his thoughts still wanted to go back to Aubrey — never wanted to leave him — it was easy to keep them focused on the job as long as he was with someone else. He and Robin talked about the dhampirs and kicked around some ideas about what to do. They were still waiting for the results of the blood work Caley had done on the latest victim, but Oren knew they didn't have time. As far as he could see, the dhampirs' goal was to kill all the vampires in the city. They couldn't possibly do that, but they could certainly try, and it seemed they were.

"Should we warn the coven?" Robin asked.

Oren blinked at him. He wasn't panting yet, but he would

eventually, and he couldn't wait for that moment. He didn't want to chat. He wanted to run and to forget about everything. "You mean the one in town? They already know about the dhampirs."

"Sure, but maybe they don't know the details. I know vampires don't like dhampirs, but they might not be aware of how dangerous they are. Most of them seem to think they're inferior monsters, but they don't consider them dangerous." Robin looked at Oren. "But we both know that's not true. I think we should talk to the coven and any lone vampire who might listen to us. We can explain what's happening and give them tips on how to be careful."

It wasn't a bad idea. Something needed to be done. So far, the vampires who had died weren't part of the only coven in the city—the one Aubrey belonged to. Some coven leaders wanted all vampires who lived in the same town or city to belong to their coven, but Fyfe wasn't like that. He didn't want the power that came with it. He wanted to keep his coven safe, and as long as he knew who the other vampires were and where they lived, he was okay with them not being part of the coven. That meant a lot of vampires lived in the city. The city was peaceful, or at least, it had been before the dhampirs had arrived.

But the vampires needed to be protected, and the lone ones were the ones who were in the most danger . Fyfe would take care of his coven. He already was. What about the others, though?

Oren swallowed. He couldn't stop thinking about Aubrey, and he was relieved Aubrey was part of Fyfe's coven. He was an enforcer, so he might still get hurt, but he wasn't alone. "It's a good idea. Give me a list of vampires who live alone. We'll contact them and tell them what's happening," he told Robin.

Robin grinned at him. "I do have good ideas sometimes."

Oren couldn't help but smile at that. "More than sometimes. But you're right. I hadn't thought about that." Because he'd been focused on Aubrey. He wasn't doing his job the way he should.

"You have other stuff to focus on and to worry about," Robin said. "No one berates you for that. You're focused on the job, but you're allowed to take time off and not to think about it."

"Not until the dhampirs are dealt with."

Robin gave him a strange glance. "I don't think that's fair. We all have a personal life. You don't ask us to give you what we can't. You don't expect us to be at your beck and call the entire time or to be alone in life. Why should you demand that from yourself.?"

Oren didn't have an answer to that, or rather, he didn't have an answer he could give Robin. So he just gave Robin a tight smile and went back to his running.

Chapter Four

Aubrey hummed as he fed Adrian. He was cooing at the baby and tapping his foot to the sound of the music he'd put on in the kitchen, and he couldn't stop smiling.

He knew it was too early to think things were going well with Oren. Aubrey hadn't heard from him since they'd had sex almost a week ago, even though he'd waited. He thought Oren would eventually call him, and he was disappointed he hadn't. He understood why, though. Knowing Oren, he was probably overworking himself. Aubrey would be surprised if he had time to have dinner before flopping into bed and going to sleep, only to wake up the next evening and go back to work.

As far as Aubrey knew, the dhampirs still hadn't been found. It was a problem, to the point that even Aubrey was starting to worry. He didn't like knowing there was someone in the city waiting for him or any other vampire to leave the safety of their home and kill them. He didn't know what to do about it, and he knew it wasn't his job. His job was to protect the coven, and that was what he'd been doing. He and Fyfe had talked, and they'd agreed to increase the security measures. Some coven members hadn't liked it, but they couldn't deny it was necessary, not with yet another murder.

That was one of the reasons Aubrey hadn't contacted Oren. Two days after they'd spent time together, another body had been found. Aubrey knew Oren well enough to realize that he probably felt responsible for it. He wouldn't be surprised if Oren blamed *him* for distracting him or something like that, and he hadn't wanted to fight. He also hadn't wanted to distract Oren even further, but now, he was starting to wonder if he'd done the right thing.

It might be true that he was distracting, but it didn't mean it had to be a bad thing. People were dying, and Oren was overworking himself to find the killers. What would happen if he was too tired? What if the dhampirs targeted him and his team, and he didn't have the same quick reaction that he would have if he were well rested? He was obsessing over this, and it was his job to do so, but Aubrey suspected that his past meant he couldn't think of anything else. He probably felt guilty over having spent time with Aubrey, and he was avoiding him.

Aubrey wasn't sure what to do about it.

"You sound chipper," Fyfe said as he walked in.

Aubrey smiled at him. "That's because I am."

"More than usual, though. You don't normally sing to the baby while you feed him."

"I'm not singing." God knew no one would want that, considering what a terrible singer he was. "But yeah. I'm happy." Mostly. He was worried about the fact that Oren hadn't contacted him, and he realized he was making excuses for him. The only way for him to find out what was happening would be to go to Oren, though, and he wasn't sure he should do that. But he also didn't want to stay away. He wanted Oren to remember him, and spending more time away from him would make it harder. It was giving Oren time to find excuses not to be with him, even though he wanted to.

Aubrey didn't know what to do. "It's just—" he began, unsure what to say.

Fyfe took a bottle of blood from the fridge, then leaned against the counter. "You don't know what to do with Oren."

Aubrey wasn't surprised Fyfe knew about Oren. "You're right. I don't. We had sex once, and he told me he had feelings for me. He told me he was falling in love with me."

"And that's a good thing. It's why you're singing, isn't it?"

"It is, but then I remembered that he also told me we couldn't have a relationship." Aubrey sighed and cooed at

Adrian. "He thinks I'm a distraction, and he's not entirely wrong. I mean, he needs to focus on this case, and instead, he's having sex with me."

Fyfe frowned. "I get that, but life can't only be work, even when it's important. God knows I have plenty of things to do for the coven, but I still find time to be with James. I wouldn't be the man I am now, the *leader* I am now if I didn't have James by my side and didn't spend time to love him."

Aubrey grinned at Fyfe. "That's what you call it? *Love* him?"

Fyfe rolled his eyes. "You know what I mean. I understand where Oren is coming from, especially with what's happening, but I think you shouldn't allow him to push you away, not unless he was clear that he doesn't want to be with you. But eventually, this case will be over, and Oren's team will be sent away. What will you do then?"

Aubrey had thought about that. Of course he had. He'd been tempted to talk to Ignatius and Oscar about it, but he hadn't wanted to be rude and to remind them that eventually, Ignatius might have to leave. He was sure they'd talked about it, and he didn't need to know how they were going to solve it.

He was curious, though. His relationship with Oren wasn't the same as the relationship Ignatius and Oscar had. To begin with, those two were actually together, while Oren and Aubrey had merely had sex once. They might have admitted to each other that they had feelings, but that didn't mean something would come out of it. Hell, if Aubrey knew Oren, nothing would. As soon as he was done with this case, he would disappear, and Aubrey would never see him again. If he was lucky, Oren would come back to him when he was in town to have sex, but that wasn't what he wanted. If it was at all possible, he wanted a relationship with Oren.

But it looked like he was going to have to do something if

he wanted that to happen. Staying away from Oren wasn't working, and the only other thing Aubrey could do was find him.

He looked at Fyfe, then at Adrian, and grinned. "I think you should spend time with your uncle Fyfe," he said.

Fyfe sighed. "You know I don't have the time."

"He's a coven member, and he needs your help. I'm sure you'll find the time."

He knew Fyfe wouldn't mind. He loved Adrian, just like most of the coven did. It was true he didn't spend a lot of time with the baby, but that was mostly because of his duties. If he was in the kitchen, though, it meant he had a little time.

Aubrey rose from his chair and handed the baby to Fyfe. "I'll find Oscar on my way out and tell him what's going on. I'm sure he'll come soon."

"I'm not in a rush," Fyfe said as he took the baby and went back to feeding him.

Aubrey looked at them for a moment, then headed out after finding Oscar. If he was going to do this, he had to do it now.

Oren didn't like the thought of him going around the city on his own, but it was the only way for him to get to the conclave building, so he did. He drove there, tense, looking around half expecting someone to jump out of a car and try to grab him. Thankfully, nothing happened, and he reached the conclave building without a hitch. Once he was there, he felt better, though. No matter what he told Oren, he couldn't deny that the thought of dhampirs killing vampires in town made him nervous.

The guard at the door looked up when he heard the door open. "He's not here," he said before Aubrey could say anything.

Aubrey blinked. "How do you know who I'm here for?"

The guard smiled. "Everyone knows who you're here for.

But he's not here."

Aubrey looked around. He didn't want to go back, but he wasn't sure he could wait. "Do you know when he'll be back?"

"No idea."

"Can I wait?"

The guard hesitated, but just then, a man came out of one of the many doors Aubrey was curious about, and his gaze stopped on Aubrey. He grinned, and he seemed to know something about Aubrey that Aubrey didn't. He strode toward him, holding a hand out. "You're Aubrey, right?"

Aubrey no idea who this guy was, but he still shook his hand. "I am. I'm sorry, but I don't know who you are."

"Caley. I'm on my way out, but I thought you would want to know that Oren is already at the crime scene."

Aubrey blinked. "Crime scene?"

Caley's smile disappeared. "There was another murder."

The bottom of Aubrey's stomach dropped. "Another? But it's only been five days."

"Four. And like I said, Oren's team is already there. Do you want to come along with me?"

Aubrey frowned at Caley. "Are you sure? I'm not a conclave enforcer." And he was pretty sure Oren wouldn't be happy to see him.

"Don't worry about it. As long as you stay away from the crime scene and you don't touch anything, it shouldn't be a problem."

"I won't, but still."

"I'm the medical examiner. If I say it's not a problem, it won't be."

Aubrey had nothing to say to that, so he followed Caley outside. He needed to see Oren, to reassure himself the man he loved was okay. They might not be together, but it didn't mean he wasn't worried, or that he didn't care.

It was the same as the other cases, and Oren wasn't sure what to do about it. He looked around, trying to find clues without touching anything. Caley was on his way, and Oren had to be careful. If there were any clues that would tell them who was doing this and where to find them, he didn't want to fuck it up.

"Who's the victim?" he asked.

Robin looked at a notebook he was holding. "I found her wallet in her handbag. Gabriella White. I'm not sure how long she had been a vampire, but I have an address, so I'm going to contact whoever she lives with."

Oren nodded. "Be careful when you tell them what happened to her."

Robin looked offended. "Always." His gaze flickered to something behind Oren. "Caley is here."

Oren was glad. The sooner Caley could tell them what had been done to Gabriella, the sooner they could get to work and try to find her killers.

Of course, that hadn't helped in the other cases that they were working. Even though Caley had autopsied the bodies, they had no certainty. The only thing they could say for sure was that the vampires had been drugged and decapitated. There was no proof as to who had done it and why, and it was starting to get frustrating. Worse than that, it was dangerous. Oren had to do something, but what?

He turned around to greet Caley, and his eyes widened when he saw Aubrey was with him. "What the fuck?" he muttered. They were chatting as if they were at the park rather than at a crime scene, and Oren couldn't believe his eyes. It looked like Aubrey had arrived with Caley, and it didn't make sense.

He strode toward them.

Caley moved away from the van, while Aubrey stayed beside it, shuffling his feet and looking awkward.

"What the fuck are you doing?" Oren asked Caley when he reached him.

Caley shrugged. "He was at the conclave building looking for you. I told him you were at the crime scene, and I offered to bring him to you."

"Why? He's not a conclave enforcer. He has no place here, and you should know better."

Caley's expression hardened, and he straightened his back. "You're right. He shouldn't be here. But I know you've been avoiding him, and even though he's not a conclave enforcer, he knows what's going on, and he *is* an enforcer, even if it's only for his coven. He knows how to behave and not to create trouble. I'm sure of that."

"Even if I were avoiding him, you really think the solution is bringing him to a crime scene?"

Caley's expression twisted into what looked like guilt. "Okay, so maybe it wasn't a good idea. But he hasn't even stepped away from the van. He won't unless you tell him he can. Talk to him. Tell him you're okay. He's worried about you."

That gave Oren pause. "He told you he was?"

"He didn't have to. Come on. I know you want to find whoever killed this victim and all the others, and I want that, too. It's not going to happen right this minute, though. You've already gone over the crime scene, and you won't find anything else until I do my job. Go to him. *Talk* to him. I'll let you know as soon as I have anything."

Oren didn't have a choice. He couldn't ignore Aubrey, not when everyone was aware of his presence and that he was here to see Oren.

Oren moved toward Aubrey. He didn't know what he was going to tell him, but he was angry — angry at Aubrey for not giving him a choice, at Caley for bringing Aubrey to a crime scene he should never have been at.

He stopped in front of Aubrey, and Aubrey smiled at him. It made something in Oren's heart soften, but he couldn't allow it to. "What the fuck are you doing here?" he snapped.

Aubrey took a step back as if Oren had hit him. He didn't say anything, and Oren hated it.

"Answer me, Aubrey. What are you doing here? This is a crime scene. You can't be here, and it doesn't matter that you're here to see me. If I wanted to see you, I would have called you."

Aubrey flinched. "You're an asshole."

"I might be, but I'm also working, and this is important work. You can't be here to distract me. This isn't your place."

"I'm not a child. I know it's not my place, and I wasn't planning on moving away from the van. And stop yelling at me. You can tell me you're disappointed and angry without the yelling."

Jesus Christ. Oren was used to being obeyed. When he told his team to do something, they did. Aubrey never listened, though. Oren had told him he shouldn't go around on his own, yet he'd disobeyed him once again. He'd just told him he shouldn't be at a crime scene, yet he didn't look like he was going to leave anytime soon. Why was he doing that? Oren knew Aubrey didn't have to listen to him, but he was only trying to keep him safe. Couldn't Aubrey see that?

Oren gritted his teeth. "You need to leave."

"We should talk."

"We have nothing to talk about. Nothing to tell each other. You need to stay away from my crime scenes and from me."

Aubrey's expression shifted again, and while Oren couldn't read it, he could see there was pain there. He was hurting Aubrey. It was what he needed to do, though. He couldn't allow Aubrey to do this. He couldn't allow Aubrey to push and find a way under his shield. That shit was in place for a reason, and no one could break it down. Oren couldn't allow it, especially not considering the circumstances.

"You're not serious," Aubrey said.

"I'm incredibly serious. I already told you we couldn't have a relationship."

"We had sex. I told you to call me if you wanted to do it again."

"But we both know it's not the only thing we have. I can't do this, Aubrey. I can't be with you. It doesn't matter how I feel about you. Besides, I told you not to go around on your own, and you agreed to do it. Yet here you are, and I know you drove to the conclave building alone. Don't try to bullshit me and tell me it's not true."

Aubrey crossed his arms over his chest. "I wouldn't have come if you'd called me like you were supposed to."

Oren shook his head. "I wasn't supposed to do anything. We're not a couple, Aubrey. We never will be. I want you to stop calling me."

"I never even called you. I gave you time to get used to what we did, to wrap your mind around it and make a decision."

That much was true. Oren had been tempted to call Aubrey so many times, though. Eventually, he'd deleted his number from his phone. That way he wouldn't be able to call, no matter how much he wanted to. He couldn't tell Aubrey that, though. He couldn't tell Aubrey anything about how he felt about him, not anymore. He'd made his decision, and he needed to stick to it.

His job was his life. It had been his life for a long time, and it wasn't about to change, no matter how he felt about Aubrey. If this was what he had to do to keep Aubrey safe, to keep him at the coven and not going around in the city, then he would do it.

He stepped closer, and Aubrey's eyes widened. "Listen to me," Oren said. Aubrey nodded, and Oren continued. "There can be nothing between us. I shouldn't have had sex with you. I regret it, because I gave you hope when I shouldn't have. This isn't going anywhere, Aubrey. How I feel about you and how you feel about me doesn't matter. I can't do this, and I won't. I won't allow you to ruin my job."

"Ruin your job? What are you talking about?"

Oren shook his head. "You're distracting me. I should be focusing on finding this killer, but instead, I have to take care of you because you're at one of my crime scenes. Go home. Don't try to contact me. I'm sorry, but I have nothing to say to you."

Oren saw the moment Aubrey understood he was serious. He could see the heartbreak in Aubrey's eyes, and he had to resist the urge to reach for him, to tell him he hadn't meant any of that.

He wasn't sure he had. He didn't want to kick Aubrey out of his life, but he could see it was the best thing, probably for both of them. That way he would be able to focus on his job, and Aubrey would be free to find another man and build a relationship and a life with him, whoever he would be. It didn't matter that Oren was jealous of that nonexistent man. He had done what he needed to do, just like always. It was his job.

This was it. Aubrey hadn't been sure it would ever happen. He'd *hoped* it wouldn't. He'd hoped that eventually Oren would realize they could be together, that he would want it as much as Aubrey did.

Clearly, he didn't.

Aubrey didn't know if he'd said those things just because he was angry at seeing Aubrey there, but even if that were the case, it didn't matter. Aubrey wasn't sure he could forgive Oren for what he'd said.

He realized he shouldn't have been there. In hindsight, coming with Caley, even though Caley had said it wasn't a problem, hadn't been a good idea. But Aubrey hadn't been planning on talking to Oren until Oren was ready for him to. He'd planned on staying out of the way and not interrupting anyone. He'd been thrilled when Oren had noticed him and come toward him, even though Oren had been angry. It was better than being ignored.

Or at least, Aubrey had thought so. He'd felt a bit stupid, like a teenage girl with her first crush. He shouldn't have been this happy to have Oren talk to him, especially after Oren had ignored him for an entire week.

But he had been, and now his heart was crushed.

He took a step away from Oren, then another. Oren's gaze flicked to the van, and he seemed to realize there was a problem. He sighed heavily and rubbed his face. "Stay here. I'll have one of my team members take you back to your car."

Aubrey shook his head. "I don't need you to."

"Of course you do. You're here on your own, and I can't allow you to walk back to the coven, or to the conclave building. None of us should be alone around the city right now, especially not you."

That irritated Aubrey even more than he already was. "*Especially* not me? Are you saying that because I'm just a coven enforcer instead of being a conclave enforcer? I know I might not be as good as you at defending myself, but I'm not an idiot. I'm good at my job, though. So, no. I don't need anyone to drive me back to my car. I can go wherever I want on my own." He hoped he was hiding the fear and worry he felt.

He wasn't sure he could leave Oren behind. He was in love with him, even though Oren was uncompromising and serious and he wanted so much more from him—*with* him. He knew they could be good together, and he suspected Oren had reacted to a possible danger when he'd said those things to him. He was careful with Aubrey. That much was obvious.

Aubrey wasn't sure it was a good excuse, though. He understood fear, and he understood why Oren had snapped. Still, he'd said things, things Aubrey hoped he would regret, but he couldn't be sure Oren hadn't meant what he'd said. Maybe Oren truly didn't want to be with him, no matter how he felt about him. He'd told Aubrey that, and Aubrey needed to respect his words.

He shook his head and moved away.

"Aubrey! Stay here. I'll get someone," Oren said.

Aubrey paused, but he didn't turn around. He waited until he heard Oren had left, then he ran away.

He knew it was stupid and childish. He should have waited for Oren to get a team member. He didn't need Oren, though. He didn't need him, and he wanted to show him that.

He knew where they were in the city, so he was aware that he could walk home. The coven was closer than the conclave building, so he headed toward it, not wanting to go back to the conclave building. He never wanted to go back there, not when he might see Oren. He wasn't sure what it would mean for Falkner and his visits to Darren, but he doubted that was important right now. Besides, Falkner would probably understand. As soon as Aubrey told him what had happened, he would be the first to tell Aubrey to stay away.

Aubrey slowed down once he was sure he was far enough away that Oren wouldn't catch up to him. He didn't know what to do except go home. That was what Oren wanted, and now it was also what Aubrey wanted. He wanted his room, to be able to hide, to nurse his broken heart.

He still couldn't believe what Oren had said. He'd admitted he had feelings for Aubrey, so why was he still pushing him away? Was it just fear, or was there another reason, a better one? Aubrey didn't know, and at this point, he didn't think it mattered. Whatever the reason behind Oren's behavior and his words, it was obvious he meant them. It didn't matter that he was in love with Aubrey. He wasn't planning on being with him, and he'd been clear about that.

That meant Aubrey would have to stay away.

It was probably for the best. Aubrey had promised himself that while he would try to get Oren to see they could be good could together, he would leave Oren alone if Oren didn't change his mind, and he doubted that would happen. The reason didn't matter. Whether it was fear or something else, Oren had been clear. He didn't want Aubrey in his life, and Aubrey needed to respect that, no matter how hard it was.

He felt like his heart was breaking in his chest, and he reached up, touching it. It felt normal. His heartbreak wasn't physical, no matter how much it felt like it.

Aubrey huffed. Yes, he was in love with Oren. Oren wasn't the first person he'd loved to dump him, though. He would get over it, just like he always did. There was nothing special about Oren.

Except it felt like there was.

Aubrey didn't know why Oren was so special to him, and he didn't think it mattered. He couldn't help what his heart wanted, and it wanted Oren, no matter how nasty he'd been.

Aubrey still had hope, but he knew he had to ignore it. Even if Oren had said those things because he was tired, angry, or scared, it didn't change the fact that he had said them. He had known it would hurt Aubrey, yet he'd done it, and he'd gotten the result he'd expected. Aubrey's heart was broken, and he didn't know if he could put it back together, not for Oren, not right now.

Aubrey sighed. This was it, wasn't it? No matter what he

and Oren had shared until now, it was over. Aubrey had to respect that. It would be hard, but he had other things to live for. He could focus on the coven, on his friends, and on Adrian. He wasn't alone, even though he felt like it right now. That was only him being dramatic. He would get over this, over Oren, and he would be happy again, even though it would take some time.

He felt better once he'd made the decision. He couldn't force Oren to be with him, and that was okay. He would be fine.

He walked toward the coven, his thoughts preventing him from being careful, even though he knew it was stupid. Still, he noticed the car parked on the edge of the road a while before he reached it. He hesitated, wondering if he should go the other way, but a woman stepped out and waved at him. She gestured at one of the tires, and Aubrey cautiously moved closer. "Is there a problem?" he asked.

The woman was pretty—blonde, with wide eyes and a slight blush on her cheeks. She was wearing a dress and sandals, and she gestured at the tire again. "I think I have a flat tire," she said softly.

"I see. Have you called anyone?"

She shook her head. "I tried, but my phone is dead, and I never learned to change a tire on my own. I don't know what to do." Her lips trembled, and Aubrey was pretty sure he could see the sheen of unshed tears in our eyes. He didn't want her to cry. It made him feel like he was about to cry, too, and he didn't want to spill more tears for Oren.

He forced himself to smile at her. "It sounds like you're in a bit of trouble. I can help you if you want." He realized she might not want to, though. He was a man, and they were alone on the street.

She smiled at him. "You would? Oh, my God. I would be so grateful."

"Of course. I can't exactly leave you alone here, can I?" He gestured at the trunk. "Why don't you pop it open? I'll grab the spare tire. You'll be home before you can worry about it."

The woman went back into the car and obeyed. Aubrey opened the trunk to get the spare tire, and he felt movement behind him too late. It couldn't be the woman, because he could see her when he straightened, but she was the last thing he saw. Something hit him on the back of the head, and he tilted forward.

Oren caught Robin's gaze. "I need you to drive Aubrey home," he said.

For some reason, Robin glared at him. "That's not going to be possible."

Oren frowned. "Why not?"

"Because he left as soon as you turned your back on him."

Oren twirled around, and sure enough, Aubrey was nowhere to be seen. "That man. He's going to get himself killed," Oren muttered.

"From the sound of it, *you're* going to get him killed."

Oren was shocked at the way Robin was talking to him. He turned to look at him, and sure enough, Robin was still glaring. "What are you talking about?" Oren asked.

"You might not be aware of it, but the two of you were yelling. We heard what you told him, and we all saw the moment his heart broke. You're a dick, Oren."

Oren couldn't deny that. "I'm realistic. And you have nothing to do with my relationship or my love life, so keep your opinions to yourself."

"Sure thing. I just thought you should know that you're a dick." Robin stepped away without adding anything, and Oren resisted the urge to strangle him.

He was right. Oren *was* a dick, and he didn't like it, even though he knew it was necessary. Maybe he shouldn't have done this now, though. He'd sent Aubrey running, and he couldn't stop wondering if something might happen to him. Right now, Aubrey was walking the streets on his own, and he was exactly the kind of target the dhampirs went after. What if something happened to him and it was all Oren's fault?

Oren shook his head. He couldn't think that way. The dhampirs had just killed again, and there were always a few days between one victim and the next. Nothing would happen to Aubrey. Besides, Aubrey was an enforcer. Like he'd told Oren minutes ago, he could defend himself. Oren needed to have faith in that. He couldn't go running after Aubrey, not when he'd just told him to stay away. He had to follow his own rules.

He moved closer to Caley, who was working on the body. When Caley heard him, he looked up and glared at him just like Robin had. "He's not wrong," he said, tilting his chin toward Robin, who was gathering evidence further down the alley. "You *are* a dick, and you really shouldn't have talked to Aubrey that way."

"You shouldn't have brought him here. It wasn't his place."

"I already apologized for that."

"I didn't hear you apologize. You said you shouldn't have done it, but that's not an apology."

Caley's eyes narrowed. "Fine. I apologize for bringing Aubrey here. I see now that I shouldn't have. I should have realized you would be a dick to him, and he didn't deserve it. If you were angry at someone, it should have been me, not him."

Oren sighed and rubbed the back of his neck. He detested feeling like the bad guy, even when he was.

Relationships were harder than work. When he was on the

job, he knew what he could and couldn't do. He knew what he ought to do to make sure the job was done and done well. But when it came to Aubrey and love, Oren had no idea what to do. "I shouldn't have yelled at him," Oren quietly agreed. "But it's better this way. He needs to stay away from me and to stay safe, and his presence here means he's not."

Caley got to his feet and looked at Oren. "Why do you want him to stay away so badly?"

"Because it's the best thing for both of us. My job is dangerous, and he has no place in it."

"He doesn't have anything to do with your job. He was here, yes, but that was entirely my fault. I saw him waiting for you in the entrance back at the conclave building, and I told him to come along. I knew you'd been avoiding him, and it was obvious he was going to wait for you. I was wrong. I should have given both of you the time and space you needed, but I thought I was doing the right thing. I certainly didn't think you were going to blow up at him and break up with him."

Oren shook his head. "I didn't break up with him."

"It sure sounded like it."

"I couldn't have broken up with him because we were never together."

"Are you sure? Because I saw a hickey on your neck the other day."

Oren barely resisted the urge to slap a hand on his neck. "We had sex, but it doesn't mean we're in a relationship. I told him that. I told him it was only sex and that there could be nothing more between us."

"But you don't believe that, do you? Because it's obvious you have feelings for him."

Oren hated that he was so obvious. He hated even more than he'd admitted to Aubrey that he had feelings for him. He shouldn't have, but he'd thought it would help keep Aubrey safe. He should have known better. "It doesn't matter what I feel for him or what he feels for me. We can't be together."

Caley hesitated. "Is it because of Lucas?"

Everyone knew about Lucas. Oren and his team had already all been working for the conclave when it had happened, as had Caley. They'd been friends, and he'd tried to convince Oren to give Lucas more time. He'd made him see that he was overworking himself, and he'd tried to convince him there was more to life than work.

Oren had given in. He'd been about to talk to Lucas, to tell him they should try to work things out. He hadn't had the time, though. Lucas had died afraid and disappointed in him, thinking he'd lost him. He hadn't been aware of the fact that Oren was coming back to him, and he never would. He was dead, and it was Oren's fault.

Oren shook his head. "I won't be responsible for another death."

Caley put his hands on his hips. "Responsible? Were you the one who killed Lucas?"

"Of course not. And I know what you're going for, and I don't care. I might not have been the one who killed Lucas, but I was still the reason he was alone."

"Maybe. But he could have been alone even if you two were still together. He might have gone to visit a friend, to the bookstore, or anywhere else. You weren't attached at the hip even when you were together, so it didn't change anything. I know you're still in pain for what happened to him, and I understand. We've all lost someone. You can't let that tinge the way you live the rest of your life, though. Lucas wouldn't have wanted it."

Oren flinched. "I don't know what Lucas would have wanted because I can't ask him, can I?"

Caley shook his head. "I should know better than to try talking about this kind of stuff with you. You've always been stubborn, but especially so when it comes to feelings." He stepped closer and lowered his voice. "You're right. You can't know for sure what Lucas would have wanted, and you can't ask him. You knew Lucas, though. You were with him for years. You know that he would want you to be happy, to continue even without him. He wouldn't hold it against you. He would realize it wasn't your fault. He would want you to be with Aubrey."

Oren didn't know if that was the case. He wished he could be sure, but Lucas wasn't coming back. He would never tell Oren anything about this, and Oren needed to stop thinking about him. He had to focus on the job. Lucas was the past, and now, so was Aubrey.

Oren took a step back and cleared his throat. "What can you tell me about the victim?"

Caley stared at him for a moment, and Oren half expected him to push, to insist they needed to talk about this. He wouldn't be wrong. Oren could see he'd closed himself off from life after Lucas had died, and he knew it wasn't good. It was the only way he knew how to deal with things, though, and he wasn't about to change it.

He was relieved when Caley nodded. "There's nothing much to say, not beyond what you already know. I suspect she was drugged, and of course, she died by decapitation."

"You need to rush the blood work."

"I know how to do my job, Oren. I was already planning to do that. Now hush. I need to finish my examination before we take her back to the conclave building."

Oren stepped back and let Caley go back to work. It gave him too much time to think about Aubrey, though, and he needed that to stop. Aubrey was gone, and he wouldn't come back.

Just like Lucas.

Chapter Five

Aubrey's arms pulled to the point of discomfort, and he understood why when he finally managed to open his eyes.

It was hard. He felt like a truck had run over him, then for good measure, had backtracked and passed over him *again*. His head pounded, especially one sore spot at the back of it, and when he tried to reach around to touch it, he couldn't move his arms.

That was when he opened his eyes and saw he was chained to a wall.

He groaned and pulled on the chains, but of course, they didn't budge. This was one of the moments in which the powers of the vampires in the movies and books he sometimes read would come in handy. Instead, he was just a human being with a strange diet. There was nothing he could do about the chains, and he doubted he would be able to free himself. Still, he looked around, just in case.

He had no idea where he was or how long it had been since he'd been taken. Now that he thought about it, he realized he'd been stupid. He shouldn't have stopped to help that lady. He should have been more careful. He knew dhampirs were hunting vampires in the area, yet he'd been an idiot. He'd thought he was doing something good, helping a woman who was alone and in trouble, and this was what he'd gotten for it.

Oren was going to kill him if he made it out of this alive.

The room was just like he would have expected a cell to be—cement all around. The only window made it obvious he was in some kind of basement. It was high on the wall and too small for anyone who wasn't a child to pass through it. If he wanted to escape, he was going to have to go through the door, and he suspected that wouldn't be easy. Whoever had taken him, they'd made sure he wasn't going anywhere.

Which didn't make sense. If the dhampirs had taken him, why hadn't they killed him? That was what they'd done to all the other vampires they'd gotten their hands on. And if it wasn't the dhampirs, well, he had no idea what was going on. He didn't know why someone would kidnap him. He had nothing to offer, and even though Fyfe would be worried and try to help, he couldn't afford to pay thousands or hundreds of thousands of dollars as a ransom. Aubrey would be useless to his kidnappers, and he wasn't sure they knew that yet.

The sound of footsteps coming closer made him sit up. He'd been hit on the back of the head, but his entire body felt like he'd been put through the wringer. He wasn't sure why, but his neck hurt, too, as did his back. He sat against the wall, waiting for whoever was coming to see him.

The door opened, and a man came through. He startled when he saw that Aubrey was awake and took a step back. Then he straightened and acted as if he didn't care. Aubrey knew better, though. Whoever this guy was, he hadn't expected Aubrey to be awake, and he wasn't happy with that.

"Where am I?" Aubrey asked.

"Keep your mouth shut unless I tell you to speak," the man snapped.

Aubrey's smart mouth made him want to say fuck it and push the guy, but he could tell the man was on edge. Whatever was happening, Aubrey didn't like it. Hell, if the guy pacing the room was a dhampir, he probably wanted to kill Aubrey without asking questions.

But apparently, they wanted information. That was the only reason it would make sense for them to take Aubrey instead of killing him in the street. Aubrey wasn't sure what to think about that. He was happy he wasn't dead yet, but if these guys wanted information, they probably wouldn't hesitate to torture it out of him if he didn't talk—and he wouldn't, because he didn't know anything.

Aubrey looked at the man, waiting for him to ask whatever he needed to ask. He was pretty sure that once he answered—if he answered—he still wouldn't be let go. He was going to die in the end, one way or another. He didn't like that thought, especially not after the way he and Oren had left things, but maybe that was for the best. If Oren didn't care about him, he wouldn't care that he was dead.

Aubrey huffed. Of course Oren cared about him. He'd always known that. Even though Oren could be an asshole and a stubborn one at that, it didn't change that fact.

The man paced in front of Aubrey, betraying how nervous he was. Then, he stopped and faced him. "I want to know about Darren," he said. "And about the others you took."

Aubrey shook his head. "I'm not sure what you think happened to them, but when you say *you took*, you don't mean me. I had nothing to do with that."

"You're a vampire. You had to have had something to do with it."

The dhampirs had to know about the conclave. The conclave had been hunting them for thousands of years. "I am not a conclave enforcer. I don't work for them. I never have."

"You're lying. We saw you at the crime scene."

Aubrey winced. Going there was a spectacularly bad idea, wasn't it? Of course, hindsight was twenty-twenty and all that. "I was there, but I have nothing to do with the team investigating the murder. I was only there to talk to someone, and once I did, I left, which is when you took me. I have nothing to do with the conclave, and I don't have answers for you. The only thing I can tell you for sure is that Darren is alive. He's being treated well, but that's it."

"You're a liar. He's dead, isn't he? They all are."

"I don't know about the others. The only one I can tell you

about is Darren, because my friend Falkner visits him regularly. I don't know what was done to the others, and frankly, I don't care."

The punch came so fast that Aubrey didn't have time to move away. He doubted he would have anyway, because being chained to the wall made it so that he couldn't move easily. It hit the side of his face, making him jerk back. He didn't want to give the man satisfaction, so he didn't cry out. He was pretty sure there was blood trickling down his mouth, but he limited himself to grinning at the man.

It had a result he wasn't expecting. The man's eyes widened, and he took a step back as if he expected Aubrey to jump up and bite him. Aubrey was tempted, even though it had been a long time since he'd bitten anyone. He wanted this man to hurt, though. He'd killed all those vampires, and he was planning to kill Aubrey. H deserved to pay, as did his little friend who had played Aubrey.

The man pointed his finger at Aubrey. "Stop lying, because it won't end well for you. Give us the answers we want, and we might let you go."

Aubrey snorted loudly. "You're not going to let me go. You killed all the other vampires. Why would I be the exception?" He chuckled, shaking his head. "I'm not an idiot. I was stupid when I stopped to help your friend, but I suppose that's a better reason to die than giving you answers. You won't get anything out of me. You wouldn't get anything even if I had the answers you seek, but I don't. I have *nothing* to do with the conclave, no matter what you saw. I have nothing to tell you, and you can torture me, but it won't change that. Really, it would be a bother. You should probably kill me now." Aubrey wasn't looking forward to it, especially with the way he'd left things with Oren, but it would be better than being tortured. He didn't like pain, and if he could do without, well, he would take that chance.

The man looked like he wanted to pound Aubrey's face into the ground, and maybe he did. Maybe he *would*, and everything Aubrey was saying was only making things worse. It wouldn't be the first time it happened, and Aubrey hoped it wouldn't be the last, either.

"Tell me about Darren," the dhampir said again.

"Are you stupid? I just told you I had nothing to say to you about him or the conclave."

The dhampir punched Aubrey again. Apparently, this was how things would go, and Aubrey wasn't looking forward to it.

Oren was walking into the conclave building when his phone rang. He sucked in a breath, hoping against all odds it was Aubrey. But he knew Aubrey wouldn't call him, not after the way he'd behaved, not after what he'd said.

He'd regretted his words the second he'd realized Aubrey had left, but there was nothing he could do about it. He'd said those words, and now he had to deal with the consequences.

It was better this way. It was what he'd been trying to convince himself of since Aubrey had left, but for some reason, he couldn't seem to make himself believe it. Yes, Aubrey needed to stay away from him. He had to focus on the job, and eventually, he would leave. But long-distance relationships were a thing, weren't they?

Besides, that wasn't the only way they could make this work. Ignatius and Oscar would have to find a way, and Oren and Aubrey could, too. And while it was true that Aubrey was a distraction Oren couldn't afford right now, the case wouldn't last forever. Eventually Oren would catch the dhampirs, and he would deal with them. Then he would have more time for Aubrey, and they might be able to have something.

Or they might have been able to if Oren hadn't fucked things up.

He reached for his phone, his fingers slightly trembling. It wasn't Aubrey, though. It was Ignatius, who Oren had just sent home. Oren frowned, wondering if something had happened, and answered. "Is everything okay?"

There was a pause, then Ignatius said, "I'm not sure. Have you seen Aubrey?"

"Not since earlier tonight. Why?"

"Oscar and Fyfe told me he left the house to find you."

"That's when he found me at the crime scene." Oren knew he'd come to the conclave first, and that he'd stumbled upon Caley, who had brought him along. It was a bad idea, but Oren could admit he was the one who had made things worse, not Aubrey, and not Caley.

"He wasn't there long, though, was he? At least, I didn't notice him."

"He wasn't. I talked to him as soon as he arrived, and he left a few minutes later. Why?" he asked again. His heart was racing, and he could feel something was wrong.

"He's not home. He never came back, and it's not like him. I mean sometimes he spends the day out, but he always lets us know. It's almost dawn, and I'm not sure what to do. Are you sure he didn't go to the conclave building?"

"I'll ask around, but I doubt it." It wouldn't make sense. Aubrey didn't have a reason to come here, not after the way Oren had behaved. He'd told him to leave, and he'd thought Aubrey had gone home.

Apparently, he hadn't.

Oren swallowed. "And you're sure he's not anywhere in the house? Maybe in his room and you haven't noticed?"

"Oscar and Fyfe went around to look for him, but he's not anywhere to be seen. He never came back, Oren. I'm not sure what the two of you have going on, but this is serious. I know

Aubrey. He wouldn't have left without telling anyone."

"I was kind of an asshole to him. Maybe he just needs some alone time."

"Maybe. I hope that's what happened. But can we risk it, considering everything? I'm telling you—this isn't like him. He wouldn't stay out all day without telling anyone, no matter what happened with you."

He was right. Aubrey took his role as an enforcer for the coven very seriously. He wouldn't leave the coven without his protection, even though there were other enforcers. And like Ignatius had said, he would have told them if he'd decided to stay out. He might be heartbroken, but he wasn't reckless, and he wasn't an idiot. Something had to have happened, and it was Oren's fault, just like it had been with Lucas.

But in this case, there was still a chance. Oren had found out about Lucas only after Lucas had died. He had to hold on to the belief that Aubrey was still alive.

He swallowed again because his mouth dry. "Okay. I'm going to hang up, and you're going to go over the house again. Try to find him, look in the garden, in his bedroom, everywhere. I don't care who you have to bother."

"I will. But Fyfe has already done that, and he's not here."

"You have any idea where else he could be?"

"I've asked around, but the coven is his life. I'm going to call a few outside friends of his, though."

"You do that and let me know."

"What will you do?" Ignatius asked.

Oren looked at the door that led to the interrogation rooms. "I'm going to talk to Darren."

There was a moment of silence, then Ignatius asked, "You think the dhampirs took him?"

"I don't know. I hope they didn't, but we can't risk it. We can't act as if nothing is wrong. They'd been taking vampires left and right for a while, and the last time I saw Aubrey, he stormed off on his own. We can't ignore this possibility, not when it might get him killed."

Ignatius sucked in a breath. "I want to tell you everything is going to be okay, but I don't want to lie."

"Don't worry about me. Worry about finding Aubrey." Oren didn't want anyone to worry about him, not when he was probably the reason Aubrey was in this situation.

He hung up, texted the rest of his team to let them know what was happening and give them orders, then strode toward the door of the interrogation rooms. He talked to the guard just inside, telling him he needed to see Darren. He wanted answers, and he was going to get them. He didn't even care if he had to torture them out of Darren. He was done waiting. Darren had been treated well until now, and that wasn't going to change, at least not officially.

But Oren knew Darren had at least some idea of what was happening. He hadn't told anyone, maybe because he was afraid that once he did, his life wouldn't be worth anything to the conclave. That was over now, though. Oren would make sure he spilled everything, and if he didn't, well, Oren had been trained to get answers no matter what.

He tapped his foot as he waited, leaning against the wall. When the door opened and Darren stepped in, his gaze zeroed in on Oren, and he grimaced. "What happened?"

"Your friends took someone I care for." Oren pushed away from the wall and took a step closer, and Darren stepped back, clearly not wanting Oren to come anywhere near him. Oren didn't care. "I want you to tell me about these dhampirs. Don't try to bullshit me. I know you've been hiding things. I haven't pushed until now, and I should have. People wouldn't have died if I had. But now, this is personal, and I won't hesitate to hurt you if you don't give me what I need."

Darren hesitated. "You're right. I did hide some things.

Not because I don't want you to know, though."

"What is it, then?"

"What's going to happen to me once I tell you everything?"

"I don't know, and right now, I don't care. I want answers, and I'll get them." Oren hesitated. He wanted to throttle Darren for not having been honest, but he didn't blame him. He wouldn't have been in his place. "But I can tell you Falkner cares. He'll advocate for you."

"Will that be enough to save me from death?" Darren asked, his voice barely louder than a whisper.

"I don't know. My word might be, though."

Darren's gaze snapped to Oren. "And you would do that? You would save me?"

"It depends on what you have to tell me. I'm listening."

Darren waited for a moment, no doubt thinking about everything his honesty would imply. Then, he nodded. "All right. I'll tell you everything I know."

Oren sat down and listened.

Aubrey wasn't sure how he was still alive. The dhampir had beaten him, getting angry when Aubrey wouldn't give him the answers he wanted. It didn't matter how many times Aubrey had repeated that he couldn't give them to him because he didn't have them. The dhampir had continued asking, then beating Aubrey. Aubrey's entire body was painful, and he was steadily losing blood from somewhere. He wasn't sure where, and he wasn't planning on finding out. He wasn't planning on moving, period. It hurt way too much.

The dhampir paced the room. "You're in pain," he said.

Aubrey snorted, then winced at the pain that caused. "I wonder why," he drawled.

The dhampir stopped in front of him. "I wish I could kill you," he spat out.

Aubrey blinked. "Then do it. Kill me." At the very least, it would be less painful than this.

The dhampir shook his head. "I can't. I have orders."

That was news to Aubrey. "What kind of orders?" he asked, trying to sit up but failing. His stomach was on fire, and he wondered if the dhampir had ruptured something there. It was possible, given the way he'd been kicking Aubrey.

"We're going to exchange you." The dhampir crouched in front of Aubrey, grabbed his hair, and used his hold on him to tilt his head up. It hurt, too, that was the least painful thing the dhampir had done for now. "You have one of ours, and we have you. The vampires will exchange you for Darren."

That startled a laugh out of Aubrey. "They won't."

The dhampir pushed him away causing the back of his head to hit the wall. Aubrey had to blink a few times to see through the pain.

"Of course they will. You're a vampire."

"So? Don't you see? I might be a vampire, but I'm not a conclave enforcer. Hell, the conclave probably doesn't know I exist. They won't care. They wouldn't care even if I were a conclave enforcer, to be honest. They don't deal with terrorists. They don't give in to this kind of blackmail. They won't have a problem sacrificing one vampire to keep their best source of information on dhampirs. Besides, what Darren did was wrong. They're going to make sure he pays, and if I have to die for it, well, it won't be too much of a problem for them."

Aubrey couldn't help but wonder if Oren would be sad. Probably. No matter what Oren had told him, Aubrey knew he loved him. It killed him that Oren would blame himself for Aubrey's death, though. He'd already done enough of that when his ex had died. Aubrey hadn't known him then, but he knew him now, and he was sure that was what had happened. And now, it would happen again, but it would be so much worse because of the way he and Aubrey had left things. They'd yelled at each other, and Oren had told Aubrey to leave. Well, he'd told Aubrey to leave, but also to stay there so someone would drive him home. Aubrey had been in a huff, though, and he'd done whatever he wanted, which at that time had been to leave.

And now he was here. He was going to die, and Oren would blame himself. He would retreat into himself and his work even more, and Aubrey couldn't help but be sorry that he'd ruined Oren's life. Oren had seemed to be healing, even though he hadn't wanted it to be with Aubrey. Aubrey couldn't berate him for that, but he wished he could tell Oren not to worry about him. He wanted Oren to live his life, not to feel sorry or guilty.

"If the conclave refuses to give us Darren, we'll kill you," dhampir said.

Aubrey shrugged, and damn, that hurt, too. Every single movement hurt, so he probably should stay still for a bit. "They won't care," he repeated. "You're probably better off killing me now."

"You're saying that only because you're in pain. You don't want me to beat you up again."

"In part. But honestly, you're only delaying the inevitable. They won't agree to it. They don't know me, and they don't care about me. They'll sacrifice me because it's the right thing to do." Aubrey was going to die anyway, and he wanted to tell his truth to the dhampir. He sat up, and he was out of breath by the time he managed to lean his back against the wall. "The vampires you killed never did anything to you," he started.

"They were vampires. That's enough for me."

"Why? What did vampires do to you?"

"They created me."

"One of them did, sure. Does that mean we all have to pay for it? Besides, being a vampire isn't that bad."

The dhampir snorted. "Please. Don't tell me vampires don't hate dhampirs. I know that's a lie."

Aubrey winced. He'd always thought the hatred between vampires and dhampirs would be a bad thing eventually, and he was right. Dhampirs already had a hard time dealing with what they were. The last thing they needed was the hatred coming from vampires, and unfortunately, that was what they had. Instead of helping them understand what they were, helping them go through this, most vampires pushed dhampirs away. When they didn't outright kill them, they mocked and hurt them. "Not all vampires feel that way," Aubrey said.

"Are you trying to tell me you don't hate dhampirs? That you don't want all of us to die?"

"I don't. I don't have anything against you guys." Aubrey paused. "Well, not against those of you who didn't hurt anyone. One of my friends is a dhampir, and I don't care."

The dhampir looked puzzled. "The one Darren brought in? The one who lives with the coven."

Aubrey grimaced. He didn't want to bring attention to the coven, but he also thought he might have a way out through that. For whatever reason, the dhampir was listening to him. It might not be much, and he might still kill Aubrey in the end, but Aubrey needed to try. He didn't want to die. He wasn't going to go out without a fight, and so far, he hadn't been able to do much of that since he was chained to the wall. "Yes. Him. I've lived with him at the coven for decades, and he's my friend. I don't care what he is. The only thing I care about is that he's Falkner, and I love him for that. Our coven would never ask him to leave or hurt him."

"Only because your coven leader doesn't want to. I'm ready to bet that some of your coven members don't care and that they do want him to die."

He was right. Unfortunately, some of the coven members, especially the elder ones, didn't like dhampirs, werewolves, or anyone who wasn't a vampire. They'd already had to swallow a lot when James had moved in, then Oscar. And of course, there was Adrian, who was an abomination in their eyes. He wasn't just a dhampir. He was a vampire and werewolf hybrid, and that made him even worse than Falkner, who was vampire and human. They wanted everyone who wasn't a vampire to leave, and while that wasn't going to happen, they were all aware that the only reason it wouldn't was Fyfe. The coven had been lucky when he'd become the leader, and Aubrey hoped that wasn't going to change anytime soon.

"What you're asking from vampires is a lot," he tried to explain. "It's true that most of us don't act rationally when it comes to dhampirs, but what you've been doing isn't helping. How are we supposed to see you as anything but monsters when you've killed vampires who hadn't done anything? You've been tearing through the city, hurting our people. Vampires and dhampirs have been killing each other for centuries, and it won't ever stop if we don't try."

The dhampir shook his head and stepped away. "I don't care what you think. None of us do. You deserve to die for what you've done, for creating us, and we'll make sure it happens."

"Why is Darren so important to you? Why do you want to get him back?" Why hadn't he asked about the other dhampirs? It didn't make sense, and Aubrey wanted to find out. He wanted the dhampir to continue talking, to waste time so he might make it out of this alive.

The dhampir shook his head. "It's none of your business." He moved to the door, and before Aubrey could add anything, he was gone.

Aubrey slumped against the wall. He wasn't sure he'd gained anything from the conversation, but he hoped so. He wasn't dead yet, so that was a good thing.

How long would that last, though?

"We have to do something," Oren said through gritted teeth.

Milford arched a brow. "And what do you want us to do?"

Oren wanted to say the conclave should hand over Darren, but he knew better than to do that. They never would, and they didn't care that Aubrey's life was in danger.

The dhampirs who had taken Aubrey had contacted the conclave. Aubrey was still alive, but Oren couldn't say for how long, and he needed to do something. Of course, the conclave was making that almost impossible. They didn't want to deal with this, and they didn't care that Aubrey would die. As far as they were concerned, they weren't about to hand over a dhampir to his friends. Darren would become a danger to the conclave again, and they couldn't allow that to happen.

Oren understood that. He knew the only reason he was behaving this way was that he was in love with Aubrey. He wanted to save Aubrey, even though he knew it wouldn't be the best thing for the conclave. But for once, he'd had enough of thinking clearly. He'd had enough of putting his work before the people he loved. He'd already done it once, and he'd lost Lucas. He wasn't going to abandon Aubrey, not now, not ever. He didn't care what the conclave had to say about it.

He tightened his hands into fists. "All right. Don't give Darren over, then. But please. You can send my team to retrieve Aubrey."

Milford looked at him. "What if something happens to your team? We've trained you for years. You're one of our best resources. We can't allow anything to happen to you, no matter how much you seem to want to."

Damn it. Milford was the worst conclave member to deal with, and of course, he'd been the only one available when Oren had needed him. Still, since he had to deal with this, he was going to have to find a way. "My team is extremely well trained. We know what we're doing, and it won't be a difficult extraction. We already know the dhampirs have Aubrey. We can go in, take him back, and leave."

"They'll expect you."

Probably. Oren didn't care, though. "Of course they will. They've been expecting us since they got Aubrey. We can deal with that, though."

"I don't know. I don't think I want to risk the team."

Oren needed to calm down. He couldn't snap, no matter how much he wanted to. "We can't allow the dhampirs to think they'll get away with this. They might not have taken someone who works for the conclave, but they took a vampire, and the conclave's job is to protect us. All of us, not just the people who work for the conclave. Besides, the conclave's job is to punish whoever breaks the rules, and the dhampirs won't stop killing vampires, not unless we make them." He hesitated. He had one last card to play, and he wasn't sure he should play it. He had no way to know how Milford would react, and now wasn't the time to push things.

He was more than ready to leave if it was needed, though. He'd been a conclave enforcer for a while, and he liked his job. His life was different now than it had been when he'd started, though, and while he would regret leaving, it was worth Aubrey's life.

Milford took his time before answering. "On the one hand, I don't want to sacrifice your team. Like I said, we spent too much time and money training you. You're not wrong, though. We can't allow dhampirs to think they can get away with this. Even if we don't hand over their little friend, it will still be a surrender to leave a vampire in their hands." He looked at Oren, and Oren held his breath. He released it when Milford nodded. "All right. Go. Bring the vampire back. I hope your team will come back, too. You'll have me to answer to if they don't."

Oren didn't care. He knew it was a threat, and he wanted to tell Milford to shove it up his ass. Instead, he nodded and headed out.

His entire team was already gathered outside the room, and Oren faltered. He looked at them, knowing why they'd come. They realized how important Aubrey was to Oren, and they wanted him to know that. They wanted to help.

He had to swallow against the emotions that clogged his throat. "Let's go," he said.

They headed down the hallway, and Robin moved next to Oren. "What did they say?"

Ignatius snorted from Oren's other side. "What do you think they said? They don't care."

"Why are we going, then?"

Oren cleared his throat. "We're going because I played Milford. I told him the dhampirs were disrespecting him by taking a vampire, one of the people the conclave was supposed to protect. He didn't like that." Oren didn't care what Milford thought, as long as he'd allowed them to do this.

Robin snorted. "The guy's an asshole."

"You shouldn't talk badly about the conclave members," Oren said automatically.

Robin looked at him like he was crazy. "Fine. I won't talk badly about them. Still. I don't like him."

Oren doubted anyone liked Milford, but he didn't say anything about that. He had to focus on finding Aubrey, and he was praying the man was still alive.

Oren didn't know what he would do if he lost Aubrey, too.

He'd been horrible to Aubrey, telling him he needed to leave and that he didn't want him in his life.

He'd lied.

He suspected Aubrey already knew that, but it wasn't enough. Oren should have told him how he felt, and instead, he'd pushed him away.

"Where are we going?" Ignatius asked.

"Darren gave me the addresses of another three houses the dhampirs have been using."

Ignatius made a strangled sound. "He's known where they were this entire time, and he hasn't said anything?"

Oren nodded curtly. "He was afraid we'd kill him once we had what we wanted from him." And he wasn't wrong. Because no matter what Falkner and Oren thought, they weren't the ones in charge. They didn't give the orders.

"He allowed all those vampires to be killed."

"I know, and I'm angry at him. Now isn't the time to focus on that, though. He knows where they are and where they're most likely holding Aubrey."

"Which house are we going to?"

"I already asked another two teams to check on the ones Darren doesn't think Aubrey is at. We're taking the last one." Darren hadn't been able to give a hundred percent certainty that Aubrey was there, but he'd said it was the most probable one. That meant Oren and his team were headed there.

Oren was grateful for how cohesive and well trained his team was. They put a lot of work into this, and it showed. They didn't talk on their way to the house, and they didn't need to. They all knew what they were expected to do, what *Oren* expected them to do. They knew what was happening, and that this was a rescue mission. Oren didn't care if they killed all the dhampirs they found. As long as Aubrey was okay, he didn't care if the entire world burned down around them.

When they arrived, they parked a little away from the house. Then they filed out. They waited for Oren's orders, even though they already knew what he was going to say. He swallowed, then nodded at them. "I don't have to tell you how important Aubrey is to me. I know you've all realized that. The dhampirs took him and are using him as an exchange chip for Darren. The conclave will never allow that to happen, but they did allow us to come here to try to rescue Aubrey." Oren swallowed. "Please. Do everything you can to get to him."

They disbanded, each of them with their orders. They'd done this many times, so they knew what to do. Robin stayed with Oren, and together, they headed toward the house. Oren couldn't see the other vampires anymore, which was how things were supposed to go.

They worked like a well-oiled machine. Robin and Oren found two dhampirs guarding the front door, and they snuck behind them, killing them before they could say anything. Then they walked in through the door.

The first room was a living room. Oren heard a soft sound coming from deeper in the house, and he knew it was his team, taking care of the other guards and dhampirs. He didn't pause to ask what was going on or to check in on them. Instead, he started looking for Aubrey.

"I don't think he's upstairs," Robin murmured.

Oren agreed. One of his team members would have already found him if that were the case. They weren't just coming in from the ground floor of the house, but also from the roof.

Oren looked around and noticed a door in the hallway that led to the kitchen. "Basement?" he asked.

Robin nodded. "Probably. It would make sense."

"Let's go."

Basements were tricky. The only way in was through the

door, and they couldn't know how many dhampirs were downstairs and whether they were waiting for them. If his team was lucky, they hadn't yet realized Oren's team was in the house. If they weren't, well, this was going to be a shit show.

The basement door opened just as Oren and Robin reached it. They plastered their back against the wall behind the door, and together they waited.

A man stepped out the door and turned to close it, and Oren struck, reaching out and wrapping his hand around the man's throat. The man squeaked, but Oren had already slammed him against the wall. He slammed him again, for good measure, then handed him over to Robin and moved toward the basement door.

Chapter Six

The door slammed open, making Aubrey jerk. He hit the wall and winced at the pain. He didn't have time to dwell on it, though. The dhampir who'd been interrogating him came running into the room and slammed the door shut. His eyes were wide, and he looked around as if trying to find something. He focused on Aubrey, and Aubrey knew that whatever was happening wasn't good. At the very least, it wouldn't be good for *him*.

"How did they find us?" the dhampir asked.

Aubrey didn't want to hope, not until he was sure that whoever *they* were, they were here to rescue him. "Who?"

The dhampir shook his head. "How did you tell them where we were?"

Aubrey didn't have an answer to that. "I didn't tell anyone where we were. How could I have?"

The dhampir didn't care what Aubrey was saying, though. He'd locked the door, but someone was already on the other side of it, trying to break through. When he realized that wouldn't help, the dhampir rushed toward Aubrey. He unhooked the handcuffs from the wall, and for one second, Aubrey thought he was free. Then, the dhampir turned him around so they were back to chest and hooked an arm around Aubrey's throat.

He didn't tighten, but it was still hard to breathe. The dhampir pressed his back against the wall just as the door opened.

Oren strode through.

Aubrey's heart raced, and he tried to move toward Oren. Of course, the dhampir holding him wasn't having any of that. He kept him where he was, and to Aubrey's dismay, raised a knife to his throat. "I'll kill him if you come closer," he said.

Oren looked like he wanted to rush the guy and hit him until he fainted, but he knew better. He stayed by the door, staring at Aubrey and the dhampir. His gaze softened when he looked at Aubrey, and Aubrey couldn't help but smile at him. He winced, because even that was painful, and Oren's expression shifted again.

Aubrey could see other people behind him. He recognized one of Oren's team members, and he felt better. Oren hadn't come alone. Aubrey had no idea how Oren and his team had found him, but they were here for him, and he knew he would make it out.

Or at least, he hoped so. It would depend on the dhampir holding him.

"Let him go," someone said, and Aubrey's eyes widened. He hadn't seen Ignatius. He was surprised to see him there, considering he had a family at home, but he wasn't about to say anything about it. It was easy to forget this was Ignatius' job when Aubrey usually saw him wearing sweatpants and holding a baby.

"I won't hurt him if you let me go," the dhampir said.

"You know we can't do that," Oren said. He sounded angry, and his words slithered over Aubrey's skin, causing goosebumps. "You've been killing vampires. We have to arrest you."

The dhampir laughed, and the sound was slightly hysterical. "Arrest me? You mean kill me, just like you killed all the other dhampirs you caught."

Oren shook his head. "We didn't kill all of them. Darren is still alive."

That gave the dhampir pause. "You're lying."

"How do you think we found you? Darren told us where to find this place and another two. He told me this was where you'd brought Aubrey."

The arm around Aubrey's throat loosened. "You're lying. He would never give us up. He can't."

"I don't know what you thought you knew about him, but he's the only one who could have told me where you took Aubrey. I'm not lying. If you come with us, you can see him and talk to him."

The arm tightened again, and Aubrey sucked in a breath. He didn't like feeling this way—in pain, unable to move. Stuck. He wanted the dhampir to let him go. There would be no way out for the man. That much was obvious to everyone, even him. He was terrified, and he was trying to find a way out anyway. It wasn't like he cared about hurting Aubrey or even killing him. He'd been trying to use Aubrey as a bargaining chip, and now that he couldn't, he was holding him hostage.

Aubrey wasn't sure Oren's team would let him go, even if it meant Aubrey's death. Oren wouldn't want that to happen, of course, but he wasn't the one who made the rules. The conclave did, no matter how little Aubrey liked it. He didn't know if Oren would decide to go with his love for Aubrey or with his need to follow the rules.

He abhorred the fact that he didn't know. He wanted to be sure Oren would be there for him, but after the conversation they'd had, he couldn't. He wanted to believe in Oren, to trust that he would save him, and not being able to hurt almost as much as the bruises and wounds on Aubrey's body.

This wasn't going anywhere. The dhampir wouldn't let Aubrey go, and no matter how much Oren and Ignatius wanted to rush the guy and pull Aubrey from him, they wouldn't be able to. The dhampir's hand trembled, but he was still holding the knife to Aubrey's throat, and Aubrey didn't doubt he would use it if he had to. They were at an impasse, and something needed to change.

Aubrey sucked in a breath. He was the only one who could

do something. He had to neutralize the dhampir. If he managed to get away from him, Oren and Ignatius and the other team member who was with them could rush the guy and take him down. It would hurt, though. Right now, doing anything would hurt. Aubrey's entire body was on fire, and the arm around his throat, pulling him this way and that, wasn't helping.

He would have to save himself. He hoped Oren might let the dhampir go if that was needed to save Aubrey, but he couldn't count on that. No matter how much he disliked it, his fate was in his own hands. He had to save himself.

Luckily for him, it wouldn't be the first time he'd done it.

He wasn't an old vampire, not compared to some of the vampires he knew, but he'd had to face his fair share of people who'd wanted to kill him. Usually, they were humans who knew about vampires and thought they were demons. Sometimes, it was dhampirs or werewolves. Who it was didn't make a difference. Aubrey could still do this.

He looked at Oren, trying to tell him what he was about to do with his gaze. Oren's eyes widened, then narrowed, and he shook his head. "Let him go," he repeated. "I promise we'll let you go, too."

The dhampir snorted. "No one here believes that. As soon as I let him go, you'll kill me. I'm not going to risk it."

"What do you want, then?"

"Let both of us go. I'll allow him to leave as soon as I'm safe."

"How do I know you won't kill him?"

"You have to take my word for it."

"How can I trust you when you've been killing vampires all over town? You didn't have a reason to hurt them, yet you did. How can I trust you not to hurt Aubrey, too?"

"You can't." The dhampir's tone was harder. He pulled on Aubrey, strangling him. Aubrey knew he had to do something. "You'll have to trust me, just like I will trust you not to try to kill me," the dhampir continued.

It was Aubrey's chance. The dhampir was distracted, and Aubrey knew things would only get worse if he allowed time to pass. He took a deep breath, looked at Oren again, then moved.

He stomped his foot, relieved when he felt the dhampir's foot under his. The dhampir yelped, and Aubrey took the opportunity to elbow him. He knew it was dangerous. It would only take one movement for the knife to slide against his throat, and it did. He felt a flash of pain, then blood trickling, but he was pretty sure the knife hadn't penetrated deep enough to kill him. He turned around, pushing the dhampir's arm away, and punched him in the face. Then he moved back, stumbling and falling on his ass.

He was free, and Ignatius and the other team member who was there moved toward the dhampir. Aubrey expected Oren to do the same, but instead, Oren crouched next to him, cupping his face with both hands. "Aubrey? Are you okay?"

Aubrey closed his eyes and shook his head. He didn't know how to answer that.

Oren's first instinct was to go to the dhampir and beat his face into the ground until not even his mother would recognize him. It was hard to resist the urge, even though Aubrey was on the ground.

Maybe especially because of it. Oren wasn't sure what was happening, and he knew it was a problem. He should be the one in charge, but instead, Ignatius gently pushed him toward Aubrey while he and Robin went to the dhampir. Robin was already there, holding the man against the wall, snarling something in his ear, and Oren knew the man wasn't going anywhere. Robin and Ignatius had this. He could focus on

Aubrey.

So he went to the man he loved. He couldn't deny it anymore, and he didn't want to. The fear of losing Aubrey was the only thing he could think about right now, and his job was forgotten.

He crouched next to Aubrey and reached for him, cupping his face with both his hands, tilting it until he could look Aubrey in the eyes. He didn't want to move him more, just in case he was hurt.

Aubrey was hurt. Oren could see that, even though he wasn't a medic or a doctor. It was going to be a problem, but mostly for the dhampir who had hurt him. "How are you feeling?" he asked again. Aubrey hadn't answered the first time. He'd just stared at Oren, and Oren was getting worried.

Aubrey snorted, then winced. "Let's just say I've been better."

It reminded Oren of the time Aubrey had tripped and fallen on his face in the middle of the conclave building entrance. That was what had led them to their first kiss, and he knew they wouldn't be here now if it hadn't happened. He felt they'd come full circle, and it made him choke up. He couldn't let it show, though. He might not be acting professionally right now, but that didn't mean he wasn't the team leader.

He cleared his throat. "I bet you have been. We're going to find a doctor, okay?"

Aubrey smiled, but it was hesitant. "I think I need one this time, yes."

"Don't worry about anything. I'm here now."

Aubrey stared at Oren. "For how long, though?"

Now wasn't the moment to do this, but if Aubrey wanted to, Oren would do it. He understood why Aubrey was asking. Not only had he been tortured and beaten, but the reason he was in this situation was Oren. If Oren hadn't talked to him the way he had, if he hadn't said those things, Aubrey wouldn't be here. He might still be angry, but he would have waited for someone to drive him home, and dhampirs wouldn't have been able to find him. Instead, he'd left on his own, and this was where he'd ended up.

Aubrey tried to sit up, but Oren was pretty sure it wasn't a good idea. He attempted to push Aubrey back to the ground, but Aubrey glared at him. "The cement is cold," he said.

Oren didn't know what to do. "You might have internal wounds. You shouldn't be moving around."

"Oh, I'm pretty sure I have some. That guy was pretty dedicated when he beat me. I don't want to stay on the floor, though. It's cold, and I'm done feeling vulnerable."

Oren still wasn't happy, but he understood. He helped Aubrey sit up against the wall and did his best to ignore the grimaces and whimpers that came from him as he moved. He wanted to push and tell Aubrey he had to stop, but he knew better. Aubrey was just as stubborn as he was most of the time. Telling him he was weak wouldn't help, especially since Oren didn't believe he was. He might be in a moment of weakness right now, but no one would berate him for that.

Oren managed to hold on until Aubrey was against the wall. Aubrey was so pale that Oren feared he would faint, and he didn't know what to do. Ignatius and Robin had dragged the dhampir out, and he knew they would get the team medic. In the meantime, there was nothing Oren could do except watching Aubrey be in pain.

He hated it.

He bit his lower lip hard enough to draw blood. "I'm sorry," he murmured.

Aubrey blinked at him. "What are you sorry for?"

"For what I said to you. I didn't mean any of that."

Aubrey sighed. "I'm sorry, too. I shouldn't have come to you, especially since I knew you were at a crime scene. That doesn't excuse what you said to me, though. You hurt me."

"And I'm the reason you ended up here."

Aubrey shook his head. "Don't start thinking that way. You're not the reason I ended up with the dhampirs. They are. They tricked me into stopping. Then they grabbed me and brought me here. You had nothing to do with it."

"You wouldn't have been on your own if I hadn't told you those things."

"Maybe not today, no. But you know I wouldn't have listened to you. You know I would have continued going around on my own. Eventually, they might have found me."

That much was true. "Still. I feel guilty."

To Oren's surprise, Aubrey rolled his eyes. "Of course you do. It's what you do best, isn't it?"

"I don't understand."

"You don't because you don't see it. You feel guilty because of what happened to Lucas, and now, you feel guilty because of what happened to me, even though I was one who decided not to wait. I was the one who left on foot, and you had nothing to do with my decision."

Oren arched a brow. "We both know that's not true."

"Okay, maybe not entirely. But I could have avoided this if I'd waited for someone to drive me home. I could have avoided it if I'd waited at the conclave building instead of going to the crime scene, especially since I knew you wouldn't be happy about it. Hell, I could have avoided this if I'd waited for you to call me instead of seeking you out. You might feel guilty about this, Oren, but it doesn't mean it was your fault. If anything, it was mine."

"It wasn't. You said you were tricked into stopping."

"There was a woman. She told me she had a flat tire, and I didn't want her to be stranded on her own."

"So it wasn't your fault."

Aubrey smiled and shook his head. "We can go on like this

forever. Why don't we agree that neither of us could have stopped it? It was the dhampirs' fault, and they're going to pay for it."

Footsteps alerted them that someone was coming, and Oren acted instinctively, turning around and placing himself in front of Aubrey. The only thing he could think about was to protect the man he loved, to make sure nothing else happened to him. He didn't miss the way their team medic, Helena, blinked and looked at him. She didn't move, waiting, and it took everything Oren had to step away from Aubrey. In the end, what made it happen was Aubrey putting a hand on his back and gently pushing him away, catching his hand before he could get too far. "Let her come closer," Aubrey said. "I need her. I'm in pain."

Oren knew that. He'd known from the beginning, but that didn't make it easier. The only thing he could think about was to protect Aubrey and make sure no one came close to him. He knew it was ridiculous and that he had to stop, but he still hovered close by, just in case. Helena looked nonplussed, but she didn't say anything about it. Instead, she knelt next at Aubrey's other side and reached for him.

Oren kept Aubrey's hand in his the entire time. Oren wasn't sure which of them needed it the most. It made Aubrey feel like he was really there—like he wasn't about to fade away. Oren couldn't stop thinking about the fact that he'd almost lost him, and he didn't know what to do with himself and the feelings making his chest feel tight.

He loved Aubrey. He'd known that for a while, and now, he was even more certain of it. He knew he wouldn't be able to focus on the rest of the mission, so once Ignatius and Robin came back to check in on Aubrey, he gestured at them to come closer. "You're in charge of this crime scene," he told Ignatius.

Ignatius' eyes widened. He looked at Oren, then at Aubrey, and nodded. "Of course. Go with him."

"That's what I was planning to do." Because Aubrey wasn't going anywhere on his own, not anymore. Oren had been lucky this time. He hadn't lost him. He wasn't going to push his luck, even though they'd caught the dhampirs. It was more than that, though. He needed to be with Aubrey. He needed to tell him how he felt, how sorry he was. He had to make sure there was still a chance for them to work out, and if there wasn't, well, he would have to deal with it.

Aubrey had no idea what was going on. He knew he was safe, and that he'd been found. He knew he would heal, although that would probably take some time. No, the thing he didn't understand was what was happening with Oren.

Instead of sending Aubrey away with the medic like Aubrey had expected him to, Oren had stayed by his side. He still was. Aubrey had been stunned when he'd told Ignatius he was in charge, and he'd expected Oren to change his mind. He wouldn't have been surprised—the job was important to Oren, maybe the most important thing in his life. He'd been telling Aubrey that for weeks, and he'd been hunting the dhampirs for even longer It was the reason he'd pushed Aubrey away. He wanted to focus on catching the dhampirs, and now, he had.

Yet he didn't seem to care. Instead of going to the dhampirs and interrogating them or taking them back to the conclave building and showing off the fact that he'd caught them, he was sticking with Aubrey. He helped the medic get Aubrey out of the house, even though Aubrey had protested. He could walk, even though his knees felt like jelly. And Oren was there, wrapping an arm around his waist and holding him up as they climbed the stairs. Aubrey could hear people talking around them, walking around in the house. He was more than a little curious about Oren's decisions, and he wanted to ask *why*. Did all of this mean Oren had changed his mind? Did it mean he cared?

Aubrey wanted to hope, especially when Oren had told him he shouldn't have said the things he had, and that helped. It didn't tell Aubrey anything about whether or not they were together, though. Maybe Oren just felt guilty and still had no intention of being with Aubrey. Aubrey wouldn't be surprised. He felt like nothing could surprise him about Oren anymore, yet every time, Oren managed to surprise him anyway, just as he had with Ignatius.

Once they were settled in one of the cars the team obviously had used to get here, Aubrey looked at Oren. He was sitting next to him in the backseat, letting one of his team members drive. That was one more thing Aubrey knew was strange, and he wanted answers.

He opened his mouth to ask, but Oren shook his head. "You need to rest," he said. He was still holding Aubrey's hand, and he squeezed it. Aubrey squeezed back. He couldn't *not* squeeze back.

"I'll be fine."

Oren scowled. "You can't know that. It's why you should keep your mouth shut and rest. You need to keep all your focus and energy on healing."

Aubrey was pretty sure that wasn't how it worked, but he nodded. He might have about a thousand questions, but he was pretty tired. He felt like he'd been through the wringer, and in a way, he had. The dhampir who'd interrogated him had beaten him up pretty badly. Aubrey wouldn't be surprised if he had internal lesions, and he hoped they would get to the conclave building soon. He supposed he was lucky Oren's team had found him, and he was curious about that. How had they known where to look? Oren had said Darren had told them, but Aubrey had a hard time believing it. Why would Darren have done that?

Aubrey's eyes burned and his lids felt heavy, though, and he closed them briefly, or at least, that was what he thought.

When he opened them again, the car was parked in a garage, and Oren was gone. Aubrey jerked up, wincing at the pain. He clutched his stomach, wondering what was happening to him, when the door on his side opened. Oren was there, reaching in, and instead of allowing Aubrey to get to his feet and walk, he gathered him into his arms.

"I can walk," Aubrey insisted.

"I know you can. It doesn't mean you should. You're in pain, Aubrey. That much is obvious. Let me take care of you."

Aubrey wanted to. He wanted to allow Oren to take care of him, always. He was afraid, though. What if Oren decided he still didn't want him after what had happened? What if he didn't like the fact that Aubrey hadn't listened to him? Aubrey knew Oren was used to being obeyed, but he wasn't that kind of man. He didn't have a problem doing what Fyfe asked him to do when it came to his job, but this was different. Oren wasn't his boss. Right now, Oren wasn't anything to him, even though Aubrey wanted that to change.

He didn't know if it would.

They eventually arrived in the infirmary, and there was a flurry of activity around him. Oren had to put him down, and Aubrey let go of him, even though he didn't want to. He wanted to demand that Oren be brought back to him, but he knew better. The doctors around him were focused on making him feel better, and he had to allow them to do their job. He hoped Oren would be there when it was over, but if he wasn't, well, Aubrey would deal with that when it happened.

He was prodded and poked at for a while. Everything hurt, but the painkillers he was eventually given helped. He was relieved. He knew what the doctors were doing to him would hurt, especially when they started poking at his stomach, and he was grateful for the relief of not feeling much of that.

By the time the doctors were done, Aubrey felt like he was going to break down. He didn't want to cry, not here, not because of what the dhampirs had done, but his eyes burned, and he kept them closed, hoping everyone in the room would think he was asleep. It was tempting to do just that, but first, he had to make sure Oren had left. If he hadn't, Aubrey wanted to know why. He wanted to talk to him.

Something moved close to the bed, and Aubrey opened his eyes, already scowling. If it was a doctor, he was going to tell them to stay away from him. He'd already given them enough of his blood.

It wasn't a doctor, though. It was Oren.

He hadn't left. Aubrey hadn't realized how tense he was until he found Oren staring at him, standing next to his bed. Once he did, he finally relaxed, and he allowed the painkillers to work their magic fully. "I wasn't sure you'd stayed," he said.

Oren frowned. "What did you expect me to do?"

"I don't know. Go back to that house. I'm sure you have questions for the dhampirs."

"I put Ignatius in charge. He knows how to do his job."

"I don't doubt that. But he's not the team leader. You are, and I know how important this investigation is to you."

Oren hesitated, and Aubrey almost expected him to leave. He wouldn't have been surprised. He knew he made Oren feel vulnerable, and it wasn't something Oren was used to or that he liked. Aubrey didn't feel sorry about it, but he *did* feel sorry that it might mean they couldn't be together.

"I'm sorry," Oren said.

"You've already said that."

"I know there is no excuse for what I said. I shouldn't have been so harsh."

"Maybe it's the only way to make me understand that you don't want me." No matter how much it hurt.

Oren blinked. "That's where you're wrong. I *do* want you, more than anything."

"You didn't sound like it when you told me to go home and leave you alone. You said there could never be anything between us," Aubrey pointed out. No matter how much he wanted to ignore what Oren had said at the crime scene, he couldn't.

Oren rubbed the back of his neck. "I was angry. I was afraid for you. I was terrified that something would happen to you, and I was right."

"And it was entirely my fault, not yours. Don't start again on that, Oren. I'll slap you until you finally accept the fact that you had nothing to do with it and that the only ones who did were the dhampirs and me for not thinking things through."

Oren barked out a laugh. "All right. I won't start on that. I do feel guilty, but you're not wrong. The dhampirs were the ones who took you, and I had nothing to do with that."

"I accept your apology." Aubrey was still hurt when he thought about it, but he knew the only way they could go forward was to leave the past behind.

"I don't know why," Oren confessed. "I don't know if I could forgive myself if I were in your place. You're too good to me, Aubrey."

"I'm not too good. I'm perfect for you." Aubrey still had no idea what they were doing, though. He cleared his throat. His mouth felt dry, and he was starting to get hungry, but he wanted to get this over with first. "And I got the message. I know you care about me but that there can be nothing between us. That's okay. I'll stay away from you from now on. You won't have to tell me again, I promise."

Oren looked at him like he was crazy. "That's all you got from this?"

"I don't want to push you, Oren. You told me you didn't want me, and that's okay. It hurts, but I'll get over it."

Oren shook his head and leaned forward. Before Aubrey could say anything else, Oren pressed their lips together.

Aubrey sighed and relaxed. He hadn't wanted to hope, but it looked like he'd been wrong. He reached for Oren, trying to get him onto the bed with him, but he winced at the pain in his stomach. Of course, that made Oren move away, and it was the last thing Aubrey wanted. He finally had Oren—all of him. He would let nothing stand between them, not even his own battered body.

Oren jerked back at the whimper of pain that escaped Aubrey. He should have been more careful. He knew Aubrey was in pain, yet here he was, mauling him on his hospital bed. He was an idiot.

Aubrey reached for him, but Oren knew he couldn't do what Aubrey wanted. "You need to rest," he said.

"I need *you*," Aubrey counteracted. Even though he was obviously in pain, his gaze was steady, and he looked like a man who knew what he wanted.

"I'll hurt you," Oren said.

Aubrey shook his head. "You're not hurting me."

"I hurt you just now."

"It wasn't the kiss that hurt me. It was me trying to pull you onto the bed. If you do it yourself, I won't be in pain."

Oren couldn't help but smile. "It's your *hospital* bed. I have no business being in it."

"Please? I don't want to be alone. I want to have you close. I thought I'd lost you, and I have to reassure myself that you're not going anywhere." Aubrey hesitated. "Unless the kiss meant something else? Was it a goodbye kiss? Are you leaving for good?"

Oren didn't like that Aubrey felt this way, but he knew he'd been the one to cause it.

"I'm not going anywhere," he said, hoping the promise came clear in his voice. He wanted Aubrey to believe him.

Aubrey stared at him for a moment, then patted the mattress next to his hip. "Come on. Snuggle with me? I never got to snuggle with you, and I've wanted it for so long."

There was no way Oren could say no to that. He could tell Aubrey would push until he got what he wanted, and it was probably the best way to get him to rest.

It took a bit for them to get situated on the bed. Oren had to help Aubrey move, but he was in pain, so they had to go slow and steady. Still, he felt Aubrey relax as soon as they were together in the bed, with Oren's arm wrapped around Aubrey and Aubrey snuggled against his chest. Oren relaxed, too. He'd wanted to do this for a while, just like Aubrey, and he was relieved he still had the opportunity to do it. He'd thought he'd lost Aubrey, but he hadn't, and he would make sure he never would.

"What changed?" Aubrey asked. He sounded sleepy, and Oren expected him to fall asleep. Aubrey was stubborn, though, and apparently he wanted answers first.

"You already know about Lucas, right?" he asked as a way to start.

"I do. Ignatius told me about him, although he didn't go into detail. He just told me you lost your ex to dhampirs."

Oren kissed the top of Aubrey's head and closed his eyes. "I did. We'd been together a long time, Lucas and I. I was already a conclave enforcer when we met, and he knew how important it was to me. Still, he didn't like it. He didn't like not knowing if I was okay, if I would come home to him at night. He wanted me to quit my job and find something safer."

"But you loved your job."

Oren was grateful Aubrey knew that. "I did. I still do. I've always wanted to help people, and this is the best way for me to make that happen."

"Do you have some kind of special power like some of the other conclave enforcers?"

Oren shook his head. He knew what Aubrey was talking about. "I don't. I guess I'm just a leader." Ignatius had such a power, and he wasn't the only one on the team. Oren was just a leader, though, unless he developed his power sometime in the future. It was possible, although not probable. "Sometimes, I think the conclave is going to replace me with someone who has one, though. I wouldn't blame them. They need their tools to be as efficient as possible, and I'm just a vampire."

"You're just a vampire, but you're also good at your job. You found me."

"Because I promised Darren I would make sure nothing happened to him." Oren didn't know how he would keep that promise, but he would find a way. "I told him what was happening, and he gave me the addresses of three of the houses where dhampirs were. He already knew we wouldn't exchange him for you. I think he could tell how desperate I was."

"Tell me about Lucas?" Aubrey asked.

Oren had been sidetracked, and he knew that if he didn't push himself, he would never explain anything to Aubrey. He'd kept Lucas to himself for a long time, using the pain to keep people away. That was over, though. It had to be over if he wanted to keep Aubrey in his life, and that was what he was planning to do. "Like I said, he wanted me to quit my job. I didn't want to, though. I was making a difference, and I wanted that to continue. He got angry, and he told me that if I left the house and it wasn't to quit my job, I shouldn't come back." Oren paused, unsure whether he could go through the rest of the story. Luckily for him, Aubrey was there.

He rubbed his cheek against Oren's chest, and Oren could hear the sadness in his voice when he said, "So you did just that. You left the house, and you never went back."

Oren cleared his throat. "Exactly. I was angry. I thought he had no right to ask that of me. I still loved him, but I thought we weren't compatible, not anymore. I started to regret what I did, though. I thought we should talk about it. I was planning to call him, but I was dealing with a case, with dhampirs killing vampires, and I had to focus on that." Oren swallowed. "The next victim was Lucas. I still don't know if he would have taken me back. I never will."

"Not because of anything you did," Aubrey said. His voice was uncompromising. "I'm sorry you lost him, but you have to forgive yourself. The dhampirs killed him, not you. They would have killed him even if he hadn't broken up with you."

"I know. But the last thing I said to him was that he was selfish. I will never forgive myself for that."

"I'm sure he knew you loved him."

Oren hoped so. He'd clung to that hope for years, and he had to believe Lucas had known how much he cared for him. They hadn't been together, but it didn't mean they hadn't loved each other. They just couldn't work, not as a couple.

And now, they never would. But Oren had a second chance. He had Aubrey now, and he would make sure Aubrey always knew how he felt about him. He had to. "It's why I pushed you away in the beginning," Oren confessed. "I'd already lost Lucas to the dhampirs, and with them being in town again, I couldn't risk it."

"Yet you almost lost me to them anyway." Aubrey hesitated. "What changed? A few hours ago, you didn't want anything to do with me. Now, here you are, sharing a bed with me even though I know you didn't want to."

Oren stroked a hand down Aubrey's back. "The only

reason I told you I didn't want you was that I didn't *want* to want you. But I'm not going anywhere, Aubrey."

"Why?" Aubrey asked, and Oren knew he wouldn't be able to get him to rest. He wanted answers, and he deserved them.

"Because I almost lost you, too. I had to face the fact that even if we weren't together, it would hurt if something happened to you. It did hurt. I already lost Lucas, and I won't lose you, too. It would have been devastating if you'd died, even though we weren't together. Being with you won't change that."

Aubrey snorted. "I can't say it's the best proposal I've ever heard, but it'll do."

Oren's heart raced. "Does that mean you want me back?"

"Of course I do." Aubrey tilted his head so they could look each other in the eyes. "I've always wanted you, Oren. It might have been stupid of me, but I haven't changed my mind. I want you. I want to be with you. If you want the same thing, then I don't see what's stopping us."

Oren didn't see it, either. He kissed Aubrey, hoping he was making himself clear. Just in case, when they stopped kissing, he kissed Aubrey's forehead and nodded. "Then you have me, for however long you want me."

Aubrey laughed. "As far as I'm concerned, that's going to be forever."

And for once, that didn't terrify Oren the way it usually did.

Chapter Seven

Aubrey was feeling better, but no one believed him. It was infuriating, and he didn't know what to do about it. He felt like every time he tried to sneak out of his hospital bed, someone was there to stop him, and he was starting to be annoyed.

He wanted to go home. He *needed* to go home. He understood why Oren and the doctors had wanted to keep him close while he started healing, but he truly was feeling well. The doctors had told him it had been a close thing — the dhampir had managed to rupture something in his stomach, just like he'd thought. The doctors had told Aubrey exactly what it was, but Aubrey didn't remember. He was pretty sure he'd been high on painkillers then, but he was going to have to ask them, just in case.

He had nothing to worry about, though. Oren had been there the entire time, next to him, listening to the doctors and asking how he could help. It made Aubrey feel all gooey inside, and it had been enough to keep him nice and sweet in his hospital bed for a while.

Not anymore.

He was still in pain, but he'd had enough of the bed. He wanted to go home and see his friends. He wanted to start his life with Oren, and that wouldn't happen until Oren stopped treating him like a porcelain doll. Aubrey had been hurt, yes. He was still in pain, especially when he moved. He would get over it, though. He was well on his way to healing, and Oren and the others needed to understand that.

He looked around. He had a private room in the infirmary in the conclave building, and he didn't like that. He needed to have people around him. He disliked feeling alone, and he'd been alone since Oren had left a few hours earlier. He'd slept for a while, but he wasn't tired anymore.

He looked at the door and bit his lower lip. Oren would be pissed if he tried leaving, but then, at this point, he would probably be pissed even if Aubrey breathed the wrong way. He'd gone from not wanting Aubrey in his life to being overbearing, much like a mother hen. It was sweet, and it told Aubrey how much Oren cared for him, but it was also irritating as hell. Aubrey didn't need a mother. He'd had one, and he didn't want a second one. He needed a boyfriend, and these days, Oren felt more like a nurse than a boyfriend. He hadn't even wanted to climb into bed with Aubrey again, something for which Aubrey was still angry. Yes, he'd been wounded. That didn't mean he was going to break if Oren looked at him too hard.

He eyed the door again. This was his chance. He could sneak out of the infirmary, make his way back home, and by the time Oren would notice, it would be too late. He'd come after Aubrey, but Aubrey would be in his own bedroom, in his own *bed*, and he would be able to distract Oren. He'd tried talking to him, but it hadn't worked. Maybe it was time for something more drastic.

He got to his feet. His body felt stiff as if he hadn't moved in a while, and he hadn't. It had only been a few days, but it was a few too many days. Aubrey had never enjoyed spending time in his bed except when he had company, and this time, he didn't.

He could do this. He could walk to the door and leave the infirmary as if he was supposed to. If he did this well, no one would try to stop him, and he would be gone before Oren could notice.

His clothes had been left in the cupboard in the room. They were dirty, especially the shirt, but they would have to do. The problem was that the shirt was dirty with *blood*, and Aubrey knew he couldn't wear it to leave. It would tell everyone he shouldn't be leaving, and he didn't want someone to try to stop him.

He sighed and looked down at himself. Infirmary gown it was, then. At least he was wearing pants now.

He went to the door and swung it open, only to freeze. "What are you doing here?" he asked.

Oscar smiled at him while Adrian reached for Aubrey and babbled at him. He wanted to be in Aubrey's arms, and Aubrey wanted nothing more than to obey the silent order. He knew better than to do that, though. He was still in pain, and Adrian seemed to always hit what hurt the most.

"We came to visit you," Oscar said. He looked Aubrey up and down. "And not one second too soon, I see. Were you going to sneak out?"

Aubrey shook his head, but he knew Oscar could tell it was a lie. He looked away, and he couldn't help but smile. "Maybe? I don't want to be here anymore."

"You're whining." Oscar's tone softened. "But I understand. We all do, and we miss you, especially Adrian. Which is why when Oren came to pick us up, we couldn't say no to visiting you."

Aubrey blinked. "Oren came to pick you up?"

"I did," Oren said.

He was standing to the side, and Aubrey hadn't noticed him.

Aubrey blushed. "I wasn't leaving," he said.

"Of course you weren't," Oren drawled. He clearly didn't believe Aubrey, and he was correct.

"Okay. Maybe I was leaving. I can't stand this place anymore. I love you, but I need more than you and the doctors, and I need you to act less like a nurse and more like a boyfriend."

Oren pushed away from the door. "That's what I'm trying to do. It's why I went to pick up Oscar and Adrian. I want you to have company. I know you're going crazy."

He moved closer and gently guided Aubrey back into the room. "Now, sit down."

"I want to hold Adrian," Aubrey protested.

"It's not a good idea. I want you to see them, but I don't think you should hold the baby just yet."

"You hold him, then. I can live vicariously through you."

Oren's eyes widened, and for the first time, Aubrey thought he saw fear in his gaze. He settled on the edge of his mattress and peered at Oren. "Wait a minute. You're afraid of holding the baby."

Oren shook his head. "Of course not."

"I can see it. You're afraid of holding Adrian." Aubrey frowned. "Is it because he's a vampire and werewolf hybrid? Because he won't hurt you. He's just a baby."

Oren pressed his lips together. "It's not because of that."

Aubrey made a victorious sound. "I was right. You *are* afraid of holding him."

Oren sighed and rubbed his face. "I don't want to hurt him."

"You won't," Oscar intervened. "Sit down in the chair."

Oren looked like he wanted to argue, and Aubrey expected him to. Instead, Oren obeyed. He looked extremely uncomfortable, but he didn't say anything when Oscar stepped closer to him and handed Adrian over to him.

Aubrey half expected him to drop the baby, but instead, he settled him against his chest. Adrian stared at Oren as if he wasn't quite sure what to do with him, but eventually he seemed to realize Oren wouldn't hurt him, and he grabbed one of Oren's fingers.

Oren looked delighted. He glanced at Aubrey, a smile on his face, his cheeks flushed. "He's cute," he said.

Aubrey beamed. "Isn't he? He could be my son because of how cute he is."

Oren rolled his eyes. "That's not funny." His eyes narrowed. "You just said he was a hybrid, right? Does anyone know who his parents are?"

Aubrey gaped. "I'm not his father. I was just joking. I don't have children."

Oren laughed. "I know. I was playing with you. But you're right. He *is* cute enough that he could be your son."

Oscar settled on the mattress next to Aubrey and leaned against him, shoulder to shoulder. "They're cute together," he murmured.

"They are," Aubrey agreed. "I hope he'll come home with me when I leave this place."

"I'm pretty sure he will. You have stuff to talk about, though. He's a conclave enforcer."

"So is Ignatius, yet you're making it work. I know we can, too."

"You can do anything you want, Aubrey. You and Oren are welcome at the house. You just need to convince Oren of that."

Just then, Oren looked up, and his gaze locked onto Aubrey's. The way he was looking at Aubrey made Aubrey realize that maybe he wouldn't have to push him after all. It looked like Oren knew exactly what he was doing and what he wanted — Aubrey. And unless Aubrey was wrong, Oren would do everything he could to have him in his life, including moving out of this building and staying in town when his team was sent away. Aubrey didn't know how it would work, but he was sure of that.

"I asked to have my team assigned here permanently," Oren said, confirming what Aubrey was thinking.

Aubrey couldn't stop smiling. "You did?"

"The conclave agreed. They might still send us around if a case is important or time-sensitive, but for the rest, we'll stay here. It was time. Our team is one of the last that didn't have a home base. Now we do, and we can start putting down roots."

"And the conclave doesn't have a problem with that?"

"Of course not. They want us to be warriors and protect our people. What better way to make that happen than to be sure we have something to fight for?"

Aubrey had nothing to say to that. All he could do was smile. He had Oren, and hopefully, he'd have him forever.

You may also enjoy the following from eXtasy Books Inc:

False Friends
Catherine Lievens

Excerpt

The door slammed, jerking Dorran out of sleep. He opened his eyes, already scowling even though it was so early in the morning. He could tell by the light coming in through the window.

"Sorry," Eli said.

Dorran grumbled. "Not a problem."

"Try to get back to sleep."

Dorran softly snorted and buried his face against his pillow. That was easier said than done. Eli was used to getting up early to go to work. Hell, he was used to getting up in the middle of the night when he had a new case. Dorran, on the other hand, wasn't. That was one of the perks of working from home and making his own hours. He could get up when he wanted, which was what he did—or what he used to do anyway. Now, he and Eli had moved in together, and they were still trying to find a way to mesh their lives.

There was a rustling on the sheets, and Dorran opened one eye to see Princess Butterfly looking at him. He grinned and hooked an arm around the cat, dragging her closer. She purred and settled against his chest, and together, they drifted back to sleep. Dorran knew he wouldn't be able to fall deeply asleep again, though. He never could, not once he had woken up, especially when he'd woken up because of a slamming door.

Dorran rubbed his fingertips onto the cat's head. She was Eli's cat, but she loved Dorran just as much, which was a relief. Dorran had never had a pet, and he hadn't been sure what to do with her in the beginning. Now, she was already at home in his apartment, much more than Eli.

Dorran listened to Eli move in the bathroom. He smiled because even though he and Eli were still trying to find their way around each other and to settle in to living together without killing each other, he was happy. It was all he'd ever wanted since the two of them were teenagers. He'd broken up with Eli when they were kids, but he'd regretted it, even though he'd known he'd done the right thing. Things were different now, and he couldn't have been happier.

He and Eli had moved in together, and Eli's family was finally accepting Dorran. He hadn't thought it would happen, but even Eli's mother seemed to be happy with Dorran's presence in her son's life. He doubted she would throw them a wedding party or anything like that, but as it was, things were doing well.

Dorran was surprised when the next time he opened his eyes, he could tell several hours had passed. He listened, but the apartment was quiet, a sure sign that Eli was at work. The cat wasn't there, either. She was probably in the kitchen or the living room, staring out the window at the people who passed them on the street or sunning herself. Dorran had been abandoned, but he didn't blame her for it.

He stretched, pushing away the blankets. He had no idea what time it was, but from the sun streaming in through the window, it was about time to get up and start working.

He was looking forward to it. His life in the past several weeks had been a mess. There had been the move, but before that, the reunion with his father, finding out he had a kid sister, and his father being accused of murder. Angus had been innocent, but it had taken a while for things to settle down. Some days, it felt like they still weren't, but Dorran could deal with it. He'd dealt with a lot worse.

He got to his feet, stretched again, and headed to the bathroom, only to freeze when he stepped inside.

The room was a mess. Eli's pajama pants were on the floor, surrounded by wet towels. Water had sprayed out of the shower to the floor, and Dorran almost slipped in it. The only reason he didn't fall on his face was that he managed to grab the doorframe. The toothpaste was open on the sink, a white blob on the ceramic. Eli's electric toothbrush was there, too, abandoned next to the faucet instead of on its base.

Dorran gritted his teeth. This was one of the things he wasn't yet used to. He wasn't a neat freak, but Eli was a slob, and there was no denying that. It was one of the reasons they were still trying to find a way around each other. Even though Dorran didn't demand everything be perfect in the apartment, he also didn't want their home to look as if pigs lived with them. He understood Eli was in a rush when he left home in the morning, but that didn't mean he couldn't put the cap back on the toothpaste tube.

He huffed, then carefully stepped into the room, avoiding the puddles.

It took him about ten minutes to clean up. He hung the wet towels, put the pajama pants into the laundry basket, and dried the puddles. He also scrubbed the sink since it was dirty with toothpaste. The entire time, he was scowling.

He relaxed once he was done and going through his morning routine. Eli was always in a rush in the morning, usually because he enjoyed staying in bed for far too long and snoozed his alarm at least twice. He cleaned when he came home, but Dorran worked in the apartment, and the bathroom couldn't be in this state. He couldn't jump around water puddles to get to the toilet for the entire day.

Once he was done, he grabbed his phone from the nightstand. He texted Eli, pointing out that he had cleaned the bathroom. Then, he headed to the kitchen, smiling when he found there was a pot of coffee already made. It was still warm, and he took one of the mugs in the cupboard as his phone vibrated.

I'll clean up when I come home, Eli had written.

Dorran scowled at the words. I know you will. But I still have to go to the bathroom for the entire day, and I'd rather not slip in one of the puddles and break my nose.

The tree dots waved on the screen. Sorry. I'll do better next time. Eli had added a winking emoji, and Dorran found himself smiling.

He'd been angry, and he still was, in a way. He realized that both he and Eli were having a hard time, though. They were used to living alone. Dorran had been on his own since he'd left his mother's apartment to go to college, and it wouldn't be easy for him to get used to having someone else around — someone who did things in a different way and who wasn't as neat as he was. He supposed he would get used to it, though. People usually did. There were millions of couples in the world, and most of them lived happily ever after once they moved in together. Surely, he and Eli could have the same thing.

Dorran realized he would have to compromise, but he knew he could do it. He was happy with Eli, and he didn't want to lose that or to fight. Still, he couldn't be the only one who made an effort, and he would make sure that Eli knew that.

You think you're cute, he wrote.

I know I am. That's why you love me.

Dorran rolled his eyes. I certainly don't love you because you leave a mess in the bathroom in the morning.

I already told you would clean up. I'm sorry, but I was in a rush.

I understand that. I might work from home, but it doesn't mean I don't understand the needs of a full-time job, especially a job such as yours. Dorran paused, trying to find his words. He didn't want to make Eli angry, not when his own anger was already fading. But we live together now. We have to think of the other. Leaving everything as it is wasn't a problem when you lived on your own, but I have to use the bathroom for the entire day.

You're right. Again, I apologize. I'll see you when I come home, okay? I have to go.

Dorran eyed the text. Was Eli angry? He couldn't tell from the words on the screen. Stay safe, he answered.

Always. Love you.

Dorran smiled. Eli wasn't angry. They would work this out, like they always did. They might fight and grumble, but they loved each other, and that was what mattered.

About the Author

Catherine is the creator of several series, most of them paranormal, including the Whitedell Pride Series and the Gillham Pack Series. While she graduated in translation, she decided to go the writer's way because it was more fun to create her own stories and characters.

She's been living in Italy for more than twenty years, but she's a daughter of the North—Belgium to be precise—and she misses it so much that she's already planning to move back.

She loves pizza—probably too much—her son, her pets, and of course, books. She sneaks some reading time into her schedule every time she has five minutes free from writing, demands from her various pets and son, and lastly, housework.

Connect with her:

lievens.catherine@gmail.com
BookBub: https://www.bookbub.com/authors/catherine-lievens
Website: https://authorcatherinelievens.com/
Facebook: https://www.facebook.com/catherine.lievens.9
Facebook Group: https://www.facebook.com/groups/411788002341528/
Twitter: https://twitter.com/authorCLievens
Newsletter: http://eepurl.com/c-uvKn